A DEADLY REFERRAL

AND OTHER MYSTERY STORIES

ASHLEY LYNCH-HARRIS

BARRINGTON
HOUSE
Publishing

A Deadly Referral and Other Mystery Stories

© 2019 by Ashley Lynch-Harris. All rights reserved.

Published by Barrington House Publishing
P.O. Box 47803, Tampa, FL 33646
Barrington House Publishing and its books between columns logo are registered
trademarks of Barrington House Publishing.

Printed in the United States of America

Publisher's Cataloging-In-Publication Data

Names: Lynch-Harris, Ashley, author.
Title: A deadly referral and other mystery stories / by Ashley Lynch-Harris.
Description: Tampa, FL : Barrington House Publishing, [2019]
Identifiers: ISBN 9780996521079 (hardcover) | ISBN 9780996521086 (trade
    paperback) | ISBN 9780996521093 (ebook)
Subjects: LCSH: Murder—Fiction. | Theft—Fiction. | Ciphers—Fiction. |
    LCGFT: Detective and mystery fiction. | Short stories.
Classification: LCC PS3612.Y5429 D43 2019 (print) | LCC PS3612.Y5429
    (ebook) | DDC 813/.6—dc23

Library of Congress Control Number: 2019908772

For
My husband, Alex
My parents, Dr. Barrington and Mrs. Janel Lynch
&
In loving memory of my brother, Tremayne

TABLE OF CONTENTS

ONE

BEYOND A REASONABLE DOUBT

MR. HENRY CUBBAGE was a portly fellow, a man of self-indulgence and strict routine. After having served much of his sixty-seven years in that drafty law office with those wretched wooden chairs and seemingly endless piles of papers, he had retired and adapted quite easily to his new position in life.

Sinking into his leather chair at the Empire Club, with a bottle of his favorite port and being waited on by his usual server, Mr. Cubbage sighed happily as he unwrapped his wool scarf from around his neck, then rummaged through a box of truffles with his pudgy fingers.

"Mmm, yes...quite nice, quite nice indeed," he murmured.

Yes, Mr. Cubbage was a thoroughly satisfied man, and as the sun descended over the small town of Westend Bay and the fireplace warmed his bones, he resembled a large toad peering contentedly ahead through narrow, drowsy eyes.

Following his line of sight, one would find that it was settled in the general direction of the club's main entrance, where Mr. Hensley, the doorman, was opening the door for a tall woman with gaunt cheeks and thin lips. Her hair was simply styled and of a dull gray-brown color. Her dress, which was a faded shade of blue, matched her eyes and hung loosely from her body.

A tiny crinkle formed above Mr. Cubbage's brow as a sense of recognition swept over him.

How peculiar, he thought as his droopy eyelids rose. *Could that be…?* Mr. Cubbage frowned. *Yes, I'm almost certain she is… from the William Lawson case. Why has she returned?*

The doorman, in Mr. Cubbage's estimation, seemed unaffected by the woman with whom he was speaking, as though he didn't recognize her. However, one could never tell with Mr. Hensley. He was a lanky gentleman with a quiet, formal disposition and a keen eye. His expression was always one of indifference, and he spoke in such a detached, impersonal way that Mr. Cubbage felt assured of his discretion. Normally, it was a quality he admired.

Tilting his head forward, Mr. Cubbage stared at the doorman. *Such a hard man to read!*

Mr. Cubbage stiffened as the woman suddenly pushed past Mr. Hensley to search the main room, her eyes darting to each of the occupied seats before the doorman swiftly removed her from the sitting area. As the woman stormed away, Mr. Hensley returned calmly to his post, his expression just as wooden as before.

That man must play poker. Mr. Cubbage scratched his chin, his eyes narrowing as he studied Mr. Hensley's features. *I can't tell one way or the other if he recognized her—if he realizes that woman is a murderer.*

❧

"If you would pass the salt," remarked Mr. Cubbage to his nephew from across the dinner table.

Tim Downing cast a disapproving glance at his uncle. Mr. Cubbage visited his nephew once a week for dinner, and once a week they had some discussion concerning his health.

"That is your second helping, and the doctor said—" started Tim.

"Oh! Never mind what the doctor said!"

Mr. Cubbage always found his nephew a bit tiresome. Always so sensible! Why couldn't he leave a man alone to live as he pleased?

Tim leaned back. Raking his fingers through his neatly combed hair, silver strands blended with the shades of brown. Flashing a broad smile, he said, "Mother called me today—"

"Oh! You're relentless!" Mr. Cubbage snatched the breadstick from his plate and pointed it at his nephew. "That sister of mine doesn't know a thing about it. Cholesterol this, blood pressure that. I'm perfectly well, I tell you."

From behind a book rose the doubtful eyes of Mr. Cubbage's grandniece, Audrey. She was also present at dinner, but Mr. Cubbage, although fond of Audrey, had never been very good with children—or "variations thereof," as he put it when one argued that a twenty-year-old could hardly be considered a child—so he never did know what to say to them. However, he found that Audrey was always gracious in this regard and carried a book to read during his visits, and he had become quite accustomed to her quiet presence. She was not unruly and disruptive like other college students he had come across during his years in law. Audrey was respectful and well-mannered—almost as though she weren't there at all, which was a wonderful relief for Mr. Cubbage.

Abandoning his quest for salt, Mr. Cubbage cleared his throat.

"A curious thing happened at the club today," he said. "A woman visited…"

"Hmm, yes," murmured Tim as he finished the last bit of his mashed potatoes. "That *is* something, being a men's-only club."

"Stop with the condescension, Timothy. My life isn't all that dull," snapped Mr. Cubbage. "Let me finish."

Audrey smiled as she turned a page in her book.

"The woman who came to visit is a *murderer*. She murdered her husband, William Lawson, several years ago but was never convicted."

This time Tim's expression was one of genuine interest, and Mr. Cubbage took a sip of his wine, allowing himself a moment to relish his small victory.

"I don't understand, Uncle Henry," said Tim. "If she was never convicted, how can you be so convinced she murdered her husband?"

"The details of the case, that's how. You hadn't moved here yet, but the entire town followed the newspaper accounts when it happened." Mr. Cubbage drew back his shoulders. "I had a few friends in the police department, and I can tell you that the details of the investigation almost prove that she did it, but she managed to get off."

"Almost?" asked Audrey, startling Mr. Cubbage.

She peered at him through light-brown eyes as she lowered her book. Her mustard-yellow cardigan and dark-auburn hair reminded Mr. Cubbage of a fall morning.

"Er, yes..." Mr. Cubbage sniffed heartily and replied. "I'll explain, then, from the beginning."

Mr. Cubbage folded his napkin and thought for a moment. "Yes," he said slowly. "Four key people were involved in the case. Mr. William Lawson, a fairly successful businessman, and his wife, Gwen Lawson." Mr. Cubbage scratched at his round belly, a habit he had when mulling things over. "I believe the Lawsons were married only a year or two..."

"No children?" asked Tim.

"No, no kids," said Mr. Cubbage. "And the other two people involved were friends of the Lawsons—Michael Combs, a fellow businessman, and his wife, Helen. Mr. Lawson's murder occurred on the night that he and his wife held a dinner party with Michael and Helen Combs."

Tim leaned back as Mr. Cubbage explained.

"Dinner began with fresh salad. Mrs. Lawson kindly offered to serve the salad and started around the table, dishing out her husband's serving first. As she moved toward her guests, she tripped on the rug, and the entire bowl of salad scattered across the floor. Of course, she apologized, embarrassed, but mistakes happen." Mr. Cubbage shrugged. "The guests insisted Mr. Lawson enjoy his salad even though they didn't have any. They proceeded with the rest of the dinner, in which they all ate the same thing, with the exception of Mr. Lawson, of course, who also had a salad. Dinner concluded about an hour later, and Mr. Lawson remarked to his wife that he didn't feel very well. Apparently, he became weak and unable to move. His wife called the doctor (not immediately, mind you—she claimed that she didn't realize how bad his condition was at first), and within several hours, he was dead. The death, of course, was treated as suspicious. After all, it was entirely unexpected, and although

Mr. Lawson had not taken out life insurance, it was discovered that he had invested a large sum of money into several pieces of diamond jewelry. Sole possession of those diamonds was considered a possible and likely motive for the wife to kill her husband.

"And what of Mr. and Mrs. Combs, the Lawsons' dinner guests?" asked Tim.

"Not much there." Mr. Cubbage grinned as he fished a truffle from his pocket. "The business friend of his wasn't a competitor. He didn't gain from Mr. Lawson's death, and the wife barely knew him. There wasn't any motive."

"So, the police were pretty sure the wife was guilty?" asked Tim.

"That's right. An autopsy was performed, and it was discovered that the salad was actually made with 'fool's parsley'—it's a plant that looks a lot like parsley, but it's poisonous."

"Terrible," said Tim as Audrey slid her chair closer. "But it seems fairly obvious, doesn't it?"

Mr. Cubbage nodded. "That's what everyone said. The wife must have killed her husband for the diamonds. To make matters worse for Mrs. Lawson," added Mr. Cubbage, "the townspeople had already convicted her in their minds and made sure she knew it. You can imagine the tension. It wasn't long before rumors started floating around town that the police were planning on charging her for the murder."

Mr. Cubbage reclined in his chair and crossed his arms over his belly. A smug expression settled on his face as he continued.

"Mr. Lawson stored his diamonds in a safe, and after a decent grief-stricken display at the funeral, Mrs. Lawson decided to go through her husband's things. However, when she opened his safe, she discovered that the jewels were gone. Stolen! Just the empty jewelry boxes were left."

Tim slapped his knee. "The plot thickens!"

"The popular opinion," continued Mr. Cubbage, "was that in anticipation of being charged for her husband's murder, Mrs. Lawson had made up the stolen jewelry excuse to make it appear as though she wasn't gaining by her husband's death—soften up the jury once the case went to trial."

Tim grinned and stretched out his legs. "My, what a gossip you are, Uncle Henry!"

"Oh, shut up, Timothy!" Mr. Cubbage grunted and shifted in his chair. "Now, where was I?"

"The jewels were stolen," replied Audrey, her tone cheerful.

Mr. Cubbage jumped in his seat. *Goodness! How do I so easily forget that child is there?*

"Yes, thank you…" Mr. Cubbage gave a dry cough and went on. "The problem is that once the case did go to trial, jewels or no jewels, prosecutors knew that the defense would argue that many people have died by mistakenly eating fool's parsley."

Tim tipped his head from side to side. "Yes, I suppose so, but the way she dropped the salad seems a bit too suspicious."

"Again, I agree with you," said Mr. Cubbage, lifting his hands, "but *technically* both of those things truly could have been accidental, and you could sway a jury to agree if you went about it the right way. They really needed a strong case to make the murder charge stick."

Tim nodded. "Everything they had against her was just circumstantial."

"Precisely," said Mr. Cubbage. "As a result, the police continued to dig deeper. They couldn't afford to charge her with so little to go on. Eventually, Mrs. Lawson's phone records revealed that one number appeared several times over the few months preceding the murder. It was the number of the Empire

Club—*my* club. Someone had been speaking with Mrs. Lawson regularly, and that someone was a member."

Tim beamed and nudged Audrey's arm. "Uncle Henry?" he asked. "When did you say you became a member?"

Mr. Cubbage pursed his lips and strode toward the fireplace. "Do you want to hear the rest of the details or not?" he asked, resting his elbow on the mantelpiece.

"We do," said Audrey as she bit back her smile. "Really. It's all very interesting."

Tim and Audrey took a seat on the couch nearest to Mr. Cubbage while he remained standing beside the fire. His round belly cast a shadow across the wool rug, and the warmth of the fire improved his temperament enough to continue.

"Like I said, a member of the club was obviously in regular contact with Mrs. Lawson. The police made inquiries and discovered that it was a fellow by the name of Brennan Davis. He admitted that he and Mrs. Lawson had started an affair a few months earlier. The club seemed the safest place from which to call."

"Perhaps the lover managed to switch the salads, and maybe the wife didn't even know about it. Her tripping really was pure dumb luck," said Tim.

"No," replied Mr. Cubbage, shaking his head. "If Brennan killed Mrs. Lawson's husband out of some sort of misguided love, I would think he would have told her about the salad. If not, it would have been too risky. She could have eaten it and died as well."

"Okay," said Tim. "Then they were both in on it."

Mr. Cubbage tapped his fingers on the mantelpiece as he considered Tim's suggestion. "That's probably true," he decided. "Brennan Davis might have known about the murder plot and could have even supplied the poisonous plant, but he wasn't actually there to help carry it out. Mr. Hensley, our doorman, confirmed that he was at the club the entire evening, and he was sure he never saw him leave during the time that the murder—or accident—took place."

"I bet Brennan Davis stole the diamonds," said Tim, scooting forward. "Lovers tell each other secrets. Mrs. Lawson probably told him about the diamonds when they concocted their plan to kill the husband, and he double-crossed her. Mrs. Lawson didn't check the safe until after the funeral. There was plenty of time for him to break in."

"The police suspected them both," said Mr. Cubbage. "They kept an eye on them for a time, hoping one of them would lead them to the diamonds and build the stronger case they'd been hoping for. Unfortunately, nothing came of it. The police searched both their houses and didn't find anything. They searched everywhere Mrs. Lawson and Mr. Davis frequented, and even places they didn't but had been seen. They searched the club—nothing. Finally," said Mr. Cubbage, throwing up his hands, "Mrs. Lawson was charged with murder because she was the one who gave her husband the poisonous salad."

"But with no *real* evidence," said Tim, "the jury would have essentially been guessing as to whether she was guilty of intentionally murdering her husband or if it really was just a terrible accident."

Mr. Cubbage nodded. "But the key is that the jury must be convinced 'beyond a reasonable doubt' that Mrs. Lawson murdered her husband—that no other logical explanation exists. With the evidence presented, or lack thereof, the jury could not in good conscience say they felt beyond a reasonable doubt that she was guilty of intentionally murdering her husband."

"So, she went free, to be with her lover and probably to retrieve the diamonds she had stashed somewhere," said Tim.

Mr. Cubbage gave a firm nod. "That's what I think."

"No," said Audrey.

Both Mr. Cubbage and Tim turned to the young woman. Mr. Cubbage was taken aback not so much by Audrey's simple remark but rather by the tone in which she had made it.

"No what, Audrey?" asked Tim. "You sound quite definite about something."

"The conclusion…" A faint red hue tinged Audrey's cheeks. "I'm sorry, that was rude of me, but I just mean to say that Mrs. Lawson did not run off with her lover, and they certainly didn't live happily ever after with the diamonds."

Mr. Cubbage laughed. "How preposterous. I told you all the facts."

"Precisely," said Audrey. "That's how I know that Mrs. Lawson did not run off with her lover or the diamonds."

Tim leaned forward, resting his elbows on his knees. "What do you think happened?"

"First, I think Mrs. Lawson *did* kill her husband. She was having an affair, she obviously didn't love him, there were diamonds to be gained, and the salad mishap was, I agree, a bit too coincidental. Of course, I also agree that the jury had no choice but to rule 'not guilty.' She was smart, though, to use fool's parsley. The possibility of the poison having been a mistake presented a definite gray area, and one can cast quite a bit of doubt with gray areas. Had she used a clearly villainous poison like arsenic or strychnine, then there'd be no question, but a leafy salad…"

Audrey shrugged.

"But now to the point of the lover and the diamonds," she

went on. "It's ironic—she may have gotten rid of her husband, but because the diamonds really were stolen, she ultimately lost her lover. It would have been a disappointment to lose valuable diamonds, of course, but the real issue was that each suspected the other of having stolen them for themselves! Now, I suppose I'm a bit young to know much about relationships, but I imagine it's rather hard to have a relationship based on trust when you met as adulterers and plotted to kill the man whom she originally vowed to love for the rest of her life."

"That is a valid point," said Tim, a smile tugging at his lips.

"Right, so these lovers who really didn't steal the diamonds wondered if the other secretly had. They certainly couldn't live happily ever after with that hanging over their heads, and so they parted ways. The fact that Mrs. Lawson returned looking for Mr. Davis at the club confirms that they are not still together."

"That's true, I suppose," said Mr. Cubbage, "and I know that Mr. Davis hasn't been a member of the club since the scandal. Had they been together all that time, she would have known that."

"Exactly," said Audrey.

"I can also tell you," added Mr. Cubbage, "that Mrs. Lawson didn't look like she had been living a luxurious life. If she did think Mr. Davis had the diamonds, she probably came back because she needed help financially. She looked a bit desperate as she searched for him. He might have been the last resort."

"But how do you know one of them didn't steal the diamonds?" asked Tim.

"Yes," said Mr. Cubbage. "How can you be sure about that?"

"Oh, that's because the doorman, Mr. Hensley, stole them," said Audrey.

"I'm…I'm sorry," said Mr. Cubbage. "What do you mean *Mr. Hensley* stole the diamonds? That's ridiculous!"

Audrey's head tilted to one side. "Why?"

Mr. Cubbage opened his mouth, then closed it. He exchanged glances with Tim, who shrugged in response. "Because he just couldn't have…wouldn't have," replied Mr. Cubbage. "There would be no reason—"

"No reason?" Audrey's brows rose an inch. "Those diamonds could have been worth hundreds of thousands of dollars, for all we know. Even thousands of dollars might have been worth stealing to him."

"Okay, fine," said Mr. Cubbage, taking a seat across from Audrey. "Tell me how a simple doorman went about all this."

Audrey smiled. "*That's* how. You ask how a 'simple' doorman could go about stealing valuable diamonds. Doormen, cashiers, servers…these positions are often considered menial, and it seems to me that some people impose the status of the position onto the person as a whole—as though it sums them up entirely."

"Well…I only meant…" mumbled Mr. Cubbage.

"Oh, I'm not judging," continued Audrey. "My point is just that, in this case, a group of private club members may find themselves speaking freely in front of a doorman because his knowing details of their lives seems inconsequential to them. He is *only* a doorman. Combine these perceptions with the discreet atmosphere created in a private members club, and someone like Mr. Davis would have felt comfortable making frequent calls from there to Mrs. Lawson. As we already discussed, lovers tell each other everything—adulterous lovers especially, I expect."

Audrey was thoughtful for a moment, and then she remarked, more to herself than to anyone else, "I imagine, for adulterers, sharing their deepest secrets truly solidifies the depth of their love—and I bet it even helps to comfort the more guilt-prone individuals in justifying their actions."

"Aw, that is an interesting notion, Audrey," said Tim. "They probably tell themselves, 'Look how my marriage pales in comparison to this deep relationship I have with my adulterous partner.'"

Mr. Cubbage cleared his throat. "Yes—yes, I agree. Very interesting, but back to Mr. Hensley…"

"Oh, of course," said Audrey as she tucked a stray hair behind her ear. "As I was saying, I believe Mr. Hensley overheard Mr. Davis discussing all sorts of information during the many phone calls he made to Mrs. Lawson from the club. The briefest mention of diamonds might have piqued Mr. Hensley's interest, not to mention their discussions about when they intended to meet and where." Audrey leaned forward. "Or, in other words, when Mrs. Lawson would be out of the house." Audrey smiled. "I think Mr. Hensley took advantage of the opportunity, and before Mrs. Lawson or Mr. Davis knew it, he took the diamonds right out from under their noses."

"Incredible, Audrey," said Tim. "Well done! It does make sense!"

"Really, young lady," said Mr. Cubbage. "We should talk more often."

TWO

THE MYSTERY AT BOVEY CASTLE

"HE DIED LAST night in his house," said the woman, her voice rising above the sound of the trains entering and leaving London's Waterloo station. "I assume he must have died in his sleep, but it doesn't say…" The woman searched the next page in the newspaper. "No, it doesn't say."

George Benham looked over his shoulder, but no one else was behind him. Apparently, the woman was speaking to him.

"I knew him, you know," she went on, tapping the morning edition of the *Herald* with a manicured fingernail.

George Benham was not a talkative man. He was tall, in his late forties, with broad shoulders and a rather imposing figure. He'd been told on more than one occasion, however, that he had a "friendly face," and he was almost certain that it was this particular quality that was the cause of his current predicament.

George dragged a calloused hand across his day-old beard and offered a vague smile.

"Oh, you did?" he replied as the line moved forward. "The man who..." He nodded discreetly toward the small image of a round-faced man with glasses on the top of the newspaper's fourth page.

"Oh yes!" answered the woman. "His name was Richard Maynard. I was supposed to see him later today, in fact." She frowned. "Well, not just him. I'm meeting a group of people, but he should have been there too."

"I'm very sorry."

"Yes—yes, thank you." The woman leaned closer in an attempt to contend with the announcement being made over the loudspeaker and offered her hand. "I'm Dr. Estelle Heron, by the way. It's a pleasure to meet you."

George's brows rose as he held Dr. Heron's delicate hand in his, her wrinkled skin the only indication that she was older than he had originally thought.

"George Benham," he replied, lifting his eyes. Only hints of silver strands peeked through Dr. Heron's black hair, and only a few blemishes distracted from the softness of her deep-brown complexion.

"I suppose," she went on, "I didn't really *know* him all that well. But still. Shocking thing, isn't it? When someone dies."

"It is," George agreed as he shot a quick glance over Dr. Heron's shoulder. The line ahead was longer than he had realized.

Another announcement blared over the speaker as Dr. Heron's wide, curious eyes narrowed, focusing just beyond the ticket booth.

"Mr. and Mrs. Stallings!" she called, waving her arms.

A young couple in their thirties rushed over from the train station's small café.

"Dr. Heron, good morning," said the woman, a slight flush glowing under her fair skin, highlighting her freckles. She glanced at her watch. "Haven't you gotten your ticket?"

"Almost, almost."

Dr. Heron turned to George, who had quite comfortably settled back into his own thoughts, having assumed that his social obligations had now concluded. He was wrong.

"Mr. Burnham," said Dr. Heron. "These are my friends from America, Mr. and Mrs. Jason and Amanda Stallings."

"Benham," he corrected with a smile. "George Benham."

"We're all part of the group I mentioned earlier," said Dr. Heron. "The Emerald Historical Society."

Deep creases formed at the corners of Mr. Stallings's eyes as he smiled, a quality made more obvious by his deep tan. "It's a small amateur club," he added, "focused on discovering historical artifacts."

George folded his arms. "That is interesting," he replied with sincerity. "Definitely a unique hobby and—" He stilled. "You're that pro golfer, aren't you?" he asked Mr. Stallings. "You were on the PGA Tour last year."

Jason Stallings's face brightened. "That's right. You play?"

"Not well, I'm afraid," admitted George, shaking the man's hand. "But I try. I love the sport—you're quite good."

"Next, please," called the ticket clerk.

"Listen," said Mr. Stallings as the line moved forward. "They've got a hell of a course out where we're staying—Bovey Castle. You heard of it? Best golf in Devon. If you're ever headed that way—"

This was the first time George actually felt thankful for having been bestowed with such a "friendly face."

"Actually," he said, "I'm headed to Devon now. My daughter has been wanting me to take a trip to the countryside for a while—has been saying I need a break from…" George hesitated. "Long story short, I'm sort of planning as I go. Bovey Castle, though, sounds fine—it's perfect, really."

"Oh dear." Dr. Heron pursed her lips together. "They may be all booked up now. I had a tough time getting a room, and that was weeks ago."

Mrs. Stallings, who was presently applying lipstick, glanced over her compact mirror.

"He can have Mr. Maynard's room," she suggested with a shrug. "We read the paper this morning. He certainly won't need it."

"Amanda," whispered her husband with surprise.

"What?" Mrs. Stallings snapped her compact shut. "I don't see why people pretend to be sad about things when they aren't. It's a practical suggestion." Mrs. Stallings grinned and cast a piercing glance at George. "Unless," she started slowly, "you don't want to stay in the room of a man who has just died."

"I'm not the superstitious type," George replied.

"Good!" exclaimed Mrs. Stallings. "Then that's settled. You can ask for Mr. Maynard's room."

⚜

"Mr. Benham!"

George turned at the sound of Dr. Heron's voice. It was just after three in the afternoon when they arrived at Bovey Castle, and George had been walking the grounds.

"I'm glad I found you." Dr. Heron lifted up a navy-blue scarf. "Did you miss it?" she asked, handing it to him. "You left it at the front desk."

"Thanks." George grinned as he wrapped it around his neck. "I almost thought the receptionist wasn't going to give me Mr. Maynard's room," he joked. "But then you whipped out the newspaper from your bag and slapped it on the counter like you'd just killed a fly!"

Dr. Heron tossed her head back in laughter. "Well, she needed confirmation that he wasn't coming, and it got you your room, didn't it?"

George pulled the oval leather key ring from his coat pocket and twirled it around his fingers triumphantly. "Room 26" was etched in gold across the burgundy leather.

"This really is something," said George, stepping back to study Bovey Castle's carved brick detailing.

Beyond the grand arches and columns of the hotel's courtyard were dual stone stairways that had obviously been taunted for years by Nature's winds and rains. The grand steps were splattered with blotches of whites, grays, and browns as though Jackson Pollock had abandoned his canvas for stone. But where Nature taunted it also esteemed as green ivy climbed the blemished stone walls and wrapped its vines around the hard edges.

"Sarah would love to visit here," George said, flipping up his coat collar.

"Your daughter?"

George avoided Dr. Heron's gaze. "That's right," he replied. "She just turned seventeen."

Gravel crunched under George's boots as he and Dr. Heron turned from the hotel and followed the walking path into a gentle decline. Silence passed between them as they approached a small bridge flanked by tall, finely shaped hedges and with a river flowing gently beneath. Dr. Heron pulled her scarf to her chin as a gust of wind met them by the water.

"She's sick," said George suddenly, surprised at his own candor. "My daughter." He cast his eyes over a cluster of rocks and watched as the water cascaded over them in fine ripples. "But she is also a fighter," he added. "Stubborn, really—and there is the possibility of a new, specialized treatment, but it's only done in America…"

Dr. Heron picked up a pebble from the ground and skipped it across the water's surface.

"Sickness is quite a different battle than the other troubles of this world. It can't always be remedied by man, and that's a frightening thing," she replied.

"But in my daughter's case, it might be, but the cost—"

Dr. Heron nodded knowingly. "I understand. I'm an internist. Treatments aren't covered everywhere, especially specialized treatments."

Dr. Heron handed George a pebble. He heaved it as far as he could.

"Sarah always says I shouldn't fuss over her," said George. "But if I insist on doing so, I must first get away for a few days so I can return and fuss over her properly—with a bit of vigor, as she puts it." A smile tugged at the corners of George's mouth.

"Wise young woman!" exclaimed Dr. Heron.

"So, you see," said George, "I'm only here because of her."

George jumped as Dr. Heron clapped her hands.

"I have an idea," she said. "There *is* a way I can help."

"No," started George, "I didn't mean for you to—"

Dr. Heron waved her hand in front of George's face excitedly.

"Oh, never mind all that. Come to the drawing room at nine tomorrow morning."

❦

It was at half past eight the following morning when George finished his breakfast and walked across the hall to the hotel's drawing room. Soft pastel colors and intricate decorative details lined the walls and ceiling, where a large crystal chandelier served as its focal point. An open fireplace welcomed visitors, and two guests were seated before it, one of whom George recognized.

"You're right, Dr. Heron," said the other. "I wouldn't have believed it if you told me, but this..."

A tall, gaunt man sat across from Dr. Heron, his head buried in the morning paper.

"Absolutely unbelievable," he muttered repeatedly. He lowered the paper to his lap. "It says here that he was struck from behind!"

Dr. Heron noticed George enter and motioned for him to sit in an adjacent chair.

"Mr. Embry and I are discussing the death of Richard Maynard," she explained. "Mr. Embry is the vice president of the Emerald Historical Society," she added as she introduced them.

Mr. Embry lifted his pointed nose and peered through rectangular frames. He gave a short nod in greeting.

He was a striking man, both in appearance and temperament. He was tall, at least six foot four, but he appeared even taller because of his lanky frame. It was either old age or years of deep-seated insecurity that made him hunch his shoulders, drawing him just a tad closer to the height of the "average man," but George suspected it was a combination of both. His voice, however, was most striking of all, as it was the only thing that his age had failed to diminish—it was exacting, and had his body finally succumbed, George was convinced his voice would have picked him up and carried him further still.

Dr. Heron turned to George eagerly. "Apparently, Mr. Maynard didn't die in his sleep as I suspected."

"Really?" asked George, taking a seat.

"Of course, no one immediately suspects foul play, do they?" she pointed out. "And he wasn't a healthy man—at least not by the look of him."

Mr. Embry nodded and crossed his long legs.

"A very round man indeed," he mumbled, turning the page of the newspaper. "Couldn't have been the least bit healthy."

"So, if he didn't die in his sleep, how did he die?" asked George.

"Struck on the head!" exclaimed Dr. Heron.

Mr. Embry peeked over the top of his paper disapprovingly.

"I did already mention—" he began, but Dr. Heron went on.

"Mr. Benham," she stated firmly, "Richard Maynard was *murdered*."

"That's horrible," whispered George.

Dr. Heron rubbed her arms. "It is indeed, Mr. Benham. His death is also part of the reason why I invited you here this morning."

"I don't understand." Creases formed across George's forehead. "How does that relate to helping my daughter?"

"I'm getting to that," said Dr. Heron, grinning. "Our club is having a meeting here shortly, and I want to tell you a bit more about it before we begin."

"All right," said George as he rested his elbows on his knees. "I'm listening. I'd love to learn more about your club."

"Excellent." Dr. Heron took a sip of her tea and then began. "Although Richard Maynard was the owner of an auto company—it was his main business in London, selling luxury car parts—he also dabbled in other dealings, as well as had an interest in history and, more specifically, rare jewels."

"I see," said George. "So, you look for jewels."

"We do—and other interesting artifacts as well, but jewels are a major focus of ours." Dr. Heron reflected. "I think the power of jewels always fascinated Mr. Maynard. They've been worn by kings and queens, fought over by entire groups of people. Personally, I find observing people's behavior and their motives for obtaining jewels even more fascinating than the jewels themselves."

"Guinea pigs, are we?" asked Mr. Embry.

Mr. Embry, who had until then seemed entirely focused on his newspaper, was glaring at Dr. Heron. She turned to him in surprise.

"My, what big ears you have, Mr. Embry," she replied, amused.

Mr. Embry, who had always secretly possessed some angst concerning the size of his ears, muttered something under his breath and raised his newspaper once more.

Dr. Heron stood and walked toward the window, discreetly motioning for George to follow.

"What a lovely day," she called out.

Mr. Embry shifted uncomfortably in his seat, scooting his thin body forward, but to no avail. A succession of grumbles suggested he could no longer hear Dr. Heron and George's conversation (regardless of the size of his instruments), and he shrank back into the large wing chair, looking thoroughly dissatisfied.

Dr. Heron lowered her voice and continued.

"Mr. Embry can be a bit opinionated." Wrinkles formed around her eyes as she smiled. "I've found that a little distance is often necessary if you hope to have an uninterrupted conversation. Now," she went on, "back to what I was saying. Over time, our little group formed. We all work together to find the jewels and artifacts—everyone has his or her strengths, whether its research, connections, etcetera—and we split any profit made from their discovery."

"That sounds exciting," said George.

"And that's why I invited you to our meeting." Dr. Heron's face brightened. "The reason we are at Bovey Castle is to find a specific jewel, and I want you to join us in searching for it. If we find the jewel, we will either sell it to an individual collector, antique dealer, or museum. Then what I would like to do is give you a portion of my share."

"Oh! But I couldn't," shouted George.

Mr. Embry perked up.

"It's not for you, it's for your daughter," she whispered.

Warmth surged through George's cheeks as he fought back tears. "But I can't—"

"Either you take the money or I will donate it to a charity. Think about it—with Mr. Maynard's death, our share of the profits has increased, so I won't even miss it. Praise the Lord that I don't need it. As such, I've decided its best use would be to offer it to your daughter. But we have to find the jewel first."

Dr. Heron squeezed George's shoulder as he wiped the back of his hand across his eyes.

"Now, now. None of that," she said. "Are you in?"

George could only nod in reply.

"Good! Let me catch you up on what we know…"

George leaned his shoulder against the wall as he attempted to collect himself. Dr. Heron had already plunged into the details of their trip with the enthusiasm he had come to expect from her. It had been such a long time since he had met someone so genuinely selfless. Dr. Heron's laughter pulled him back to attention.

"Now," she continued, taking in a breath. "That brings us here, to Bovey Castle."

George cleared his throat.

"Right," he said, drawing back his shoulders. "What's the significance of Bovey Castle?"

"Bovey Castle," she said, "was built in 1907 and was first used as a family home. However, when the First World War began, it was converted into a convalescent home for officers. There was an officer by the name of Hugo Avery who was in the Royal 1st Devon Yeomanry. This regiment landed in Egypt in 1916. During his time in Egypt, however, Avery was taken severely ill and returned here to rest and recover. Now, you may be familiar with the British archaeologist Howard Carter, or at least his discovery of King Tutankhamun's tomb in November of 1922."

"I am familiar with the discovery," confirmed George. "King Tut—he was buried in a solid gold coffin. People still talk about it because grave robbers hadn't found it for thousands of years. It was rare to discover all of his royal possessions."

Dr. Heron's eyes twinkled, and she patted the oversized purse that hung from her shoulder. "We uncovered old documents and letters we believe suggest that while Avery was in Egypt, he discovered an amulet of a scarab beetle—its wings spread—that belonged to King Tut but had not been buried with him in his tomb. This amulet was engraved on the flat underside with hieroglyphs, but what was unusual was that it was also partially covered in gold. Was this intentional? If so, what was the significance? And why wasn't it buried with King Tut?"

"So, not only was this jewel discovered before the tomb, but it also poses other questions for archaeologists," said George.

"And questions always lead to more discoveries," said Dr. Heron. "Aside from the monetary value of the gold, the amulet's potential contribution to the archaeological community makes this artifact particularly desirable."

Glancing at her watch, she hurried on.

"Avery returned to England, but he kept the amulet a secret. We assume that he hoped to sell the priceless jewel once he grew well enough to leave the convalescent home. Unfortunately, he didn't recover."

"And since he never left," said George, "you assume the jewel is still here."

"That's right. And some of the wording in his journals is…interesting." Dr. Heron thought for a moment. "His later journal entries recall periods of incoherence, periods that, understandably, seemed to frighten him. He worried about 'not remembering where to find the most precious treasure of his life.' He immediately went on to describe various members of his family, but we think he really meant the jewel. He said 'treasure'—not 'treasures,' plural—and a few entries later, a single page was torn from his journal. It is on this page that we believe he might have left clues for himself as to where he hid the jewel."

Dr. Heron turned toward Mr. Embry, who sniffed twice with gusto and folded his newspaper. Setting it aside, he looked around the room and then at his wristwatch.

"Apparently," he said, "some of our little society's members have no regard for appointments."

"We're about to begin," said Dr. Heron as she and George returned to the sitting area beside the fireplace.

"Sorry, sorry!" called Mr. Stallings as he rushed into the room, followed by his wife. "Had to reserve a tee time. Excellent course out there!"

George took a seat as Dr. Heron addressed the group. "All right, let's get started," she said. "As you know, the rest of the members will arrive tomorrow, and we will begin our search of Bovey Castle then. In the meantime, I would like to propose that George Benham join in the search for the scarab beetle."

"Absolutely not," declared Mr. Embry. "Maynard may have been killed, but I have no desire for any new members."

Dr. Heron's response was swift. "Before you get all worked up, Mr. Embry, I have already arranged it so that *if* we find the scarab beetle, Mr. Benham will have a portion of *my* share."

"Wait, what do you mean Mr. Maynard was killed?" demanded Mr. Stallings, his dark brows rising under his cap.

Mr. Embry cast him an annoyed glance. "Don't you read the papers? Maynard is dead. Got himself murdered."

"I didn't know it was murder," whispered Mrs. Stallings to her husband. "Yesterday, the paper said—"

"Oh *really*?" interrupted Mr. Embry. "Does that really surprise any of you? The man was a moron. He was always provoking people. Besides, he never contributed to any of our expeditions—no one liked him."

"What a horrible thing to say," said Dr. Heron.

"He was meant to contribute this time, though," countered Mrs. Stallings. "He had those additional documents that might have helped us narrow down the whereabouts of the jewel."

Mr. Embry rubbed his chin thoughtfully. "Yes, you're right there."

"How did he die?" asked Mr. Stallings.

"Someone broke into his house," answered Mr. Embry. "Hit him on the head, but nothing was stolen. It was really very odd. Also, they discovered a golf ball marker by the body—one of those small, coin-size markers." Mr. Embry held up two skeletal fingers about half an inch apart. "They don't believe it belonged to Maynard."

Mrs. Stallings's small nose crinkled. "How odd that they'd even notice that," she remarked. "And how do they know it wasn't Maynard's?"

"Well, I don't think Maynard ever played golf," replied Mr. Embry. "The police have to question everything."

"You're wrong about the break-in," corrected Dr. Heron. "The news article said there *wasn't* forced entry. No one broke into his house. Maynard must have let the person in. He must have known his murderer."

A thoughtful expression came over Mr. Embry's face. "Now that is interesting," he said.

Mrs. Stallings fiddled with a loose earring. "What is?" she asked.

"The fact that Mr. Maynard—the one who had the most information about the location of the jewel—was killed the night before he was supposed to arrive here to find it."

"You don't mean..." muttered Mrs. Stallings, her earring slipping from her hand. "That one of us..."

Silence fell over the members of the Emerald Historical Society.

❧

After the meeting, George spent the rest of his day walking the grounds and exploring the hotel. The meeting that morning had concluded on a positive note. Dr. Heron had been successful in guiding the conversation back to the search for the scarab beetle, and the group agreed that he could take part since it wouldn't affect their share of the profits. However, George could tell that Mr. Maynard's murder, and Mr. Embry's remarks, in particular, were in the back of everyone's minds. He was not surprised, therefore, when dinnertime approached and he found himself in the midst of another excited discussion concerning Mr. Maynard's death.

"Perhaps a sordid love affair gone wrong," suggested George.

"A love affair?" exclaimed Mrs. Stallings. "Clearly, you didn't know the man."

"Perhaps it had to do with his business," proposed her husband.

"Maybe," said George doubtfully, "but it's hard to imagine anyone caring about car parts or metal tins enough to kill him."

"I still hold to my original opinion," said Mr. Embry. "Anyone could have killed Mr. Maynard, but I know our group certainly had motive!"

"Why do you keep insisting that one of us did it?" asked Mrs. Stallings, tossing her napkin onto the table.

"Because it's a valid possibility! And why?" Mr. Embry raised one of his bony hands and rubbed the tips of his fingers together. "For the money, of course—only possible reason. If we do find the scarab beetle, our share will have gone up considerably. And what if someone else is next? More deaths mean more money for those who survive!"

George studied the group. No one seemed shocked by the idea. Perhaps they had already had the same thought.

Mr. Embry took a bite of his rib eye and chewed heartily. "Stupid of him, though—the killer—murdering Maynard. He had the information we needed."

"'Him'?" asked Mrs. Stallings.

Mr. Embry shrugged his hunched shoulders. "Or her—just a figure of speech. I haven't the least idea who did it." He looked down at his plate. "Excellent steak…"

Mr. Stallings shook his head. "I don't know. I realize people have killed for large amounts of money—or even less—but it's just so hard to believe that anyone in this group would do such a thing."

"Everyone is too decent?" asked Dr. Heron, speaking for the first time.

"That's right," said Mr. Stallings. "I admit, everyone has their flaws, but not once have I thought of the people in *this* group as being capable of doing something so evil."

"You make an interesting point." Dr. Heron's lips parted into a small smile. "So, let's consider the power that a beautiful, shiny jewel can have on a human mind."

"What do you mean?" demanded Mr. Embry. "You're not talking mystic mumbo jumbo, are you?"

"No, not at all. I'm speaking scientifically." Dr. Heron slid a ring from her finger and held the diamond to the light, turning it slowly. "Did you know," she asked, studying the diamond, "that our motor cortex is stimulated when we see something beautiful?"

The other members exchanged glances.

"What that means is that we are literally compelled to reach out for whatever it is that looks so appealing." A glimmer of excitement flashed in Dr. Heron's eyes. "Are any of you familiar with the ventromedial prefrontal cortex?"

"You know we aren't," said Mr. Embry. "Come now, break it all down for us. Get on with it."

Dr. Heron grinned and pointed to her head. "There's a small cluster of neurons in our brains that assigns an object its worth and determines the depth of our emotional attachment to it." She leaned forward. "It also plays a role in our assessment of morality."

"You mean," started George slowly, "if we see something of great value—like the jewel—that cluster of neurons—"

"The ventromedial prefrontal cortex," said Dr. Heron, nodding.

"Yeah, right—that makes us experience emotion, our mind assigns a value to it, and depending on how great that value is to us, it could impair our moral judgment?"

"Precisely!" Dr. Heron threw up her arms. "Don't you see? I'm convinced that the human condition is such that, given certain circumstances—a severely agitated emotional state, for instance, or extreme emotions of love, hate, jealousy, etcetera—anyone, even a perfectly decent person, is capable of anything..."

✺

After dinner, George said good night to the rest of the group, who returned to their rooms at the other end of the hall. As he unlocked his door, the gold writing on the key ring caught his eye once more: "Room 26." Glancing down the hall again, George's pulse quickened as it suddenly occurred to him that Mr. Maynard's room wasn't with the others.

"Mr. Maynard," he considered aloud as he entered his room and shut the door firmly behind him, "had some additional information about the location of the jewel—something that no one else knew—and he specifically booked this room..."

A surge of adrenaline rushed through George.

"Of course," he murmured. "It has to be here."

He started with the closet. Hurriedly, he moved from one part of the room to the next, refusing to leave anywhere unexplored. He checked under the bed and searched the desk for secret hiding places. He pulled back the curtains and felt the fabric for hidden stitching; he even lay across the bathroom floor to check under the stand-alone tub. Still, he found nothing.

He started back at the door and moved inch by inch down the wall, feeling the bricks from top to bottom. Standing on the desk chair, he could reach the highest bricks, and he pulled back the furniture from the wall to reach the rest. Moving to the windows, he drew back the curtains and began the process again.

Halfway up the wall, he stilled. His breath caught in his throat. One of the bricks shifted slightly as he pressed his palm against it.

George grabbed a small pocketknife from his luggage and jabbed at the mortar. Bit by bit, the sealant crumbled. It took another half an hour before he finally tugged the brick free.

He coughed as a cloud of dust stirred up from the small rectangular cavity. It was pitch black, and George hesitated before sticking his hand inside. Grabbing the lamp from the desk, he propped it up on the chair beside him. With the inside of the small cavity illuminated, he didn't see anything that looked like a jewel. George reached in, feeling the walls of the cavity, cringing as cobwebs and tiny pieces of brick brushed over his hand. His fingers rose and fell as he dragged them across the coarse surface until suddenly he felt something smooth.

Something flat was resting on the bottom.

With his pocketknife, he carefully slid the blade underneath the object and inched it around the corners. The stiff object popped up. It was a thick, folded sheet of paper. Time had tarnished it, but it was still in one piece.

George's fingers trembled as he gently unfolded it, dust and broken pieces of brick sliding to the floor as he did so.

"A letter," he murmured. "No, a journal entry."

One of the sides of the paper was jagged as though it had been torn from a book or, more specifically, as George suspected, from Hugo Avery's journal. He stood and paced the room, his hands shaking. Taking a deep breath, he finally looked over the text. It was handwritten—the lettering was a bit jagged and the black ink was faded, but it was legible. It wasn't dated at the top and it began midsentence. It read:

—another day. As I look out my window, I see the trees, but the birds don't rest in their branches. I wonder what can be more valuable than freedom, soaring in the air and sky? I would never be able to soar as they do, but once I am well, I will set them free to fly.

George's shoulders fell and he slowly read the words again.

"'As I look out the window,'" he murmured, "'I see the trees...'"

George looked out the window. There were hundreds of trees! He dragged his hand through his hair as his eyes returned to the paper.

"'...but the birds don't rest in their branches. I wonder what can be more valuable than freedom, soaring in the air and sky?'"

Creases formed across George's forehead. Glancing out the window again, he shifted his eyes from the trees to the grounds, then to the grand stairway he had admired earlier that day. He knew by the condition of the stone that it must have been there since the hotel was first built—long enough to have been there when Avery stayed in this very room. From this angle, George could see half of the steps. He followed them up to the terrace and stopped. His hand tightened around the velvet curtain, which crumpled in his fingers.

Perched on the top railing of the stairway was a stone statue of a bird.

George cupped his mouth to keep from shouting.

"It's in the bird," he whispered.

He jumped from his seat and punched the air with his fists. He could barely breathe.

"The jewel is still there," he said, pressing his face against the window. "And I'm going to set the bird free."

⤸

The following morning, Dr. Heron rushed up the hotel's grand stairway and passed two hotel staff members sweeping up pieces of broken stone. Turning into the drawing room, she threw up her hands.

"Mr. Embry. There you are!"

Mr. Embry, who had fallen asleep by the fireplace, snorted and jerked awake.

"What's happened?" he yelled. "Not another one?" He stared wide-eyed at Dr. Heron as she ran into the drawing room. "Dear me, I'm next!"

"No," she said, waving her hands. "No, I need you to tell me if the news report you read on Mr. Maynard mentioned anything about his metal tins business."

"What?"

"The paper, Mr. Embry," she demanded, rummaging through a copy on the side table.

"His business?" he asked, patting down a patch of hair that was standing up on one side. "No. The reports just mentioned that he owned a successful business in London." He straightened. "Why? What's the meaning of this? Bursting in here and—"

"I didn't see it either," she said as she slumped into a chair. "Don't you get it? George Benham knew about not just one but *both* businesses that Mr. Maynard owned. It only just occurred to me that he mentioned it at dinner, but it was never reported in the papers, and I only mentioned his main business, the auto parts company."

"So, what are you saying?" asked Mr. Embry.

"George Benham must have known Mr. Maynard, and why else would he have hidden that fact unless…"

"Unless he murdered him?"

Dr. Heron allowed her head to fall into her hands.

"If George Benham did kill Mr. Maynard, then he would have found all the documents about the jewel and about this place," said Mr. Embry.

Dr. Heron lifted her head. "Then that means his arrival here was never by chance. He was heading here one way or another. He was after the jewel."

"Where is he? Let's confront him," ordered Mr. Embry.

Dr. Heron stood. "We can't. I already spoke to the receptionist. He checked out early this morning."

❧

George stared out the window of the train as it headed back to Waterloo station. The beautiful, rolling green hills were just shadows behind the faint reflection of his face that peered back at him in the early hour of the morning. He hardly recognized himself.

"Ticket, please."

George turned from the window and offered a tired smile to the ticket collector. "Here it is."

A small object clattered against the table.

"Sir," said the ticket collector as he returned his documents. "You dropped this."

The young man held out a small golf ball marker that had fallen from George's pocket.

"Bovey Castle?" asked the ticket collector, having noticed the design. "Excellent course they have there."

"Thanks," said George, taking the small marker between his fingers. "I lost mine a few days ago and needed to buy a new one."

"Play a round for me, sir," replied the ticket collector as he nodded and exited the coach.

George closed his eyes and placed his hands in his pockets. With one hand, he felt the smooth ball marker between his fingers. With the other, he traced the shape of a beetle wrapped in a handkerchief.

⌘

A Letter from George Benham to Dr. Estelle Heron
From Mallwood Prison

Dear Dr. Heron,

By now, of course, you must have realised the true extent of my actions, and I do not expect understanding—either from you or from my daughter. I would never have thought I was capable, but the human condition, as you know, is a flawed and fragile thing. I had always, until that moment in Mr. Maynard's house, considered myself a decent man.

I respect you a great deal, Dr. Heron, and I wanted to at least explain to you what happened on that horrible evening. As you must have realised, I did know Richard Maynard, and when you made my acquaintance at the train station, I was not only running from what I'd done—having murdered him the night before—but I was also running to Bovey Castle. You see, I also knew about the jewel…and its value.

The night before we met, I had just finished another long shift at Mr. Maynard's auto parts company. I worked for his company for over twenty years. Recently, I had been working as many hours as possible in an attempt to earn money for my daughter—to pay for her new treatment, which, as I told you, is costly and only available in America. But even with all the hours I worked, I couldn't afford it.

I tried to get a loan from the bank, but I had already mortgaged our home and sold everything of value. In desperation, I went to Mr. Maynard's house. I thought that having worked for him for so many years, and with his considerable wealth, perhaps he would be willing to provide money for the treatment. I would pay it back, of course. As you are aware, he was not always known for his compassion, but I had no other options.

When he answered the door, he was naturally surprised to see me. He was busy, he told me. He was packing for a trip. I saw his research about the jewel beside his suitcase and even the name of your organisation, but I didn't think much about it at the time.

I told him about my daughter. He vaguely recalled hearing of her illness. I explained, almost through tears, that there was a possibility she could be saved with a new treatment and medication. He did seem to think about it for a moment, but he was shocked by the cost. I told him I would pay back every penny. I said he could even take it directly from my pay as assurance, but he declined. And that was his perfect right.

I accepted his decision—I really did—but when he turned his back to me, I heard him laugh. Dr. Heron, I can't even explain to you the rage that went through me in that moment. What could possibly have been so amusing to this man that in such a horrible moment in my life, he could laugh? I asked him. I practically yelled, demanding that he tell me what he found so funny.

He turned back around, but he was surprised to see me there. In his mind, I had already been dismissed! He told me he wasn't laughing at me or my predicament (his words), but he found it amusing how much pharmaceutical companies could charge.

"I think I'm in the wrong business," he said.

Again, words fail to express what came over me when I heard his remark. As I look back on that moment, I can honestly say that I won't ever be able to judge another person's actions again. Desperation, the depths of one's emotions, the question of sound mind—these are powerful factors which I never considered until I met myself there, teetering on the edge of all three.

I can barely recall my actual movements, but I picked up the nearest object—it was a bronze statue, the figure of a serpent climbing a branch—and I struck him! I still can't believe what I did! But I had done it…and I had to think quickly.

I cleaned off any prints from the statue and took the notes about the jewel. I didn't know my golf ball marker had fallen from my pocket, but when I heard that they found it at the crime scene (that day in the drawing room), I didn't panic because I knew they couldn't trace it back to me. I wear a glove when I golf. It is just by chance that I've never needed to touch it with my bare hand, so I knew my prints weren't on it—but what a near miss!

I'm sure you have realised that I reviewed Mr. Maynard's information about the jewel, and I knew I had to go to Bovey Castle to find it. If the information was correct, the cost of the jewel would more than cover Sarah's treatment. I took the next train from Waterloo station. That, of course, is where I met you. Everything from then on seemed to work in my favour.

I had worried about showing up to Bovey Castle with plans to take Mr. Maynard's room—perhaps someone would have suspected something. But without meaning to, you and the Stallings provided the opportunity I needed. By being a part of your group, I was not suspected.

I tell you all this, but please understand that I did not want to deceive anyone, especially you, and when you offered part of your share of the jewel for my daughter, my heart broke as I thought of your selflessness and what I was doing… and had already done.

I shouldn't have stolen the jewel from you or the other society members, but I had already gone so far—I had already done the unthinkable. I couldn't risk the publicity your society would undoubtedly receive from the find. I had to sell the jewel quickly and quietly before the police connected the murder back to me. It made sense at that point to take the whole lot and ensure my daughter had the money to cover every treatment she'd ever need.

I'm not writing expecting you to forgive or even understand my actions, but I wanted to apologise to you nevertheless. I'm sorry for having killed Mr. Maynard, and I am sorry for having deceived you. It wasn't right. None of it was intended, but I'm not sorry my daughter lived.

Dr. Heron, she lived…

THREE
TAMARIND LODGE

THE AGED STREETLAMP cast the wavering shape of my shadow across the wet asphalt as the road curved ahead. Fatigued, my steps grew clumsy as I carried my two suitcases. I couldn't help but wonder if I had made the right decision to relocate from the United States to rural Jamaica to practice medicine. This place—Lucea, which I used to visit as a child—seemed worn now and only offered me a faint smile. Still, I readily breathed in the breezy ocean air, and as I turned onto a narrow stone path, I absorbed anew the lush vegetation of the island, which was tinted bluish green in the moonlight.

I continued on, adjusting my luggage as I walked across the uneven stones, and a faint creaking momentarily reached my ear. The sound soon came again, but this time, it was steady and drawn. I hesitated as I peered ahead, and then I noticed a tattered and crooked sign dangling on rusted hinges. I strained to make out the faded words: "Tamarind Lodge."

Pulling a worn letter from my pocket, I nodded. This was my hotel. The tarnished sign swayed once more, seeming to murmur in agreement.

I climbed the concrete steps to the hotel and mused about the places I used to visit. I pondered whether the courthouse clock still worked, and as I knocked against the mahogany door, I wondered, what of *this* place? My memory of the hotel was vague, and yet…there was *something*.

Slowly, the hotel door crept open. I saw first the soft, brown, wrinkled skin of a woman and then the rise of her prominent cheekbones as she spoke.

"I've been expecting you," she said. "Dr. Harrington Finch?"

"I am Dr. Finch," I confirmed, but as our eyes met, I was slightly startled by her seemingly cold and scrutinizing stare.

"Won't you come in?" she asked, stepping aside.

I paused on entering as I caught a glimpse of a shadow moving swiftly across the dimly lit foyer.

"Did you…" I looked toward my host. "Did you see someone…pass through the foyer?"

"Not at all," she replied as she turned her back to me. "This way, Dr. Finch."

Her walk was slow yet purposeful as she guided me down a narrow hall lined with doors. With each step, the floorboards seemed to whisper knowingly among each other of my arrival.

Clearing my throat, I remarked, "Dr. Phelps has informed me that he already made arrangements for my stay with you, Ms.…?"

"Mrs. Cuttleberry."

My step faltered at the sudden intensity with which this elderly woman turned her eye upon me.

"Cuttleberry," she repeated, slowly, deliberately.

I struggled to understand the significance.

"Dr. Rick Layton and Dr. Wendy Pruit have already arrived," she remarked, walking on. "I believe they've already gone to bed, but I can inform them of your arrival, if you'd like." She slowed as she came to a door near the end of the narrow hallway.

"No, no. Please don't," I said. "I wouldn't want to disturb them."

"Yes," she said slowly. "How considerate of you."

An almost indiscernible smirk crept across her face, but it vanished as quickly as it had appeared.

"Room number eight," she said, pressing her weight against the door. With a bit of a jolt, the door opened and Mrs. Cuttleberry gestured for me to enter. My shoulders fell as I stepped into a clean but bare room with a small secondhand hospital bed, its starched white linen firmly tucked in at its corners.

"We serve breakfast between eight and nine, Dr. Finch."

"Yes," I replied, my manner admittedly brusque. "I look forward to it, Mrs. Cuttleberry."

Her brittle nails grazed against my palm as she pressed a key into my hand. Then, stepping into the hallway, she turned and added with some amusement, "I must say, I didn't expect to see you again, Dr. Finch. Not here of all places."

"Have we met?" I asked.

"It's no matter now," she replied, turning toward the vacant hallway. "You rest up, sir. It's no matter now."

❧

The following morning, I made a point to arrive early at the hospital.

"Dr. Phelps, it's a pleasure to see you again," I remarked.

I smiled warmly as my father's old friend approached me, his dress shoes moving swiftly across the scuffed linoleum floor of Lucea's public hospital. I suddenly realized that I felt strangely displaced in the sparsely equipped building, but I soon found reassurance in Dr. Phelps's welcoming presence.

"Dr. Finch, the pleasure is all mine!" he said, grasping my hand firmly. Resting his elbow against the lobby's front desk, he reflected, "I think the last time I saw you was at your father's funeral. When was that? *Ten* years now?"

Dr. Phelps shook his head as he handed the administrative clerk a stack of patient files.

"My, how time has gone by," he remarked. "Never understood why you never came back sooner, Harrington—especially with all the land your father left you."

"I'm beginning to wonder myself," I replied, smiling.

A deep, steady laugh rumbled from Dr. Phelps's chest, only fading when his eye caught one of the nurses moving quickly through the lobby.

"Oh! Nurse Peckleton!" called Dr. Phelps, waving toward the stout, middle-aged woman. "Come meet our newest physician, Dr. Harrington Finch."

Nurse Peckleton toddled hurriedly in my direction, her gray linen nurse's dress creasing snugly on her frame.

"I'm glad you've come," she said, slightly breathless. "You've come back after many years in the States, I hear."

"I have," I replied. "I'm glad to be back."

"Must have been exciting, the land of opportunities, being able to travel and live abroad," she said, placing a folded set of bedsheets under her arm. "Are you all settled now?"

"For the most part," I replied. "I'm staying fairly close to the hospital—Tamarind Lodge. I find its location convenient, and I—"

I paused as Ms. Peckleton's gaze became suddenly distant.

"Nurse Peckleton?" I asked, casting a questioning glance toward Dr. Phelps.

Ms. Peckleton's eyes fluttered into focus.

"Oh—oh, I'm so sorry…"

Dr. Phelps looked equally concerned.

"I didn't mean to be so rude," she started. "It's just…well, when you mentioned Tamarind Lodge…" The nurse stiffened, and the crisp, starched sheets crumpled under her arm. "My father was once a guest there, Dr. Finch, many, many years ago—and that was the last time anyone ever saw him."

"I'm so sorry," I replied.

Nurse Peckleton sighed. "I can't help but feel that it was that *place*, Dr. Finch… Tamarind Lodge. It somehow had something to do with his disap—"

"Doc!"

The hospital's main door swung open, its wooden frame rattling loudly as the door collided to a stop against the wall. A man was lumbering in through the entryway. He was of average height with a worn shirt hanging from his broad shoulders. I noted a slight limp in his gait as he approached, and he was gripping his right arm tightly.

"If you'll excuse me," said Ms. Peckleton as she rushed behind Dr. Phelps toward the man.

"Doc! My shoulder's out again. Was cutting down some coconuts for Mrs. Gerzel and slipped. Same shoulder as last time." The man winced. "Me can't take this pain."

Dr. Phelps leaned forward to inspect the arm, and the man drew back.

"No, boss man," he said. "Me know something's torn this time."

"Joseph, you know how this works," replied Dr. Phelps. Removing his glasses, he rubbed the bridge of his nose. "You must first check in, and we will call you as soon as we can."

A few patients who were waiting to be seen peered through the doorway of the adjacent waiting area.

"But this is an *emergency*! If me can't use my arm, how me gon' work? I've got three jobs lined up, and if me can't use my arm, me don't get paid."

"Nurse Peckleton," Dr. Phelps started, his tone apologetic. "We haven't had any other severe cases come in since Mrs. Edwards, have we?"

"No, Dr. Phelps. The rest are minor injuries."

"Okay." Dr. Phelps rubbed thoughtfully at his chin, the shortly cropped gray hairs scratching against his fingers. "It appears that Mr. Durant might have dislocated his shoulder again. Would you please show him to an available room?"

"Of course."

Ms. Peckleton turned toward the patient as Dr. Phelps returned to me.

"You can't imagine how thrilled I am that you finally accepted my invitation," he remarked. "To be quite frank, I don't think I could have managed another year without more help. The situation here is less than ideal—as I tried to express in my letter."

"I recall," I said, nodding.

"We're severely underfunded, Harrington, and I've got just a handful of nurses and no other physicians. Thankfully, Dr. Layton and Dr. Pruit arrived yesterday, but they don't officially start until next week. I might lobby for them to start sooner!

However," he added, leading me toward the exam rooms, "I am a bit nervous. The few doctors who have come have ended up going to one of the larger hospitals hours away. Understandably so, with all their additional resources, but we just can't afford such a loss."

"Dr. Layton and Dr. Pruit are here for that very reason—as am I, Dr. Phelps," I reassured him.

"Good man," he said, patting me on the back. "We wish we could offer you more."

I raised my eyebrow as Dr. Phelps hesitated.

"As far as Tamarind Lodge," he remarked slowly, "I hope the accommodations are all right. I expect they're not what you're accustomed to, but it's all we have in proximity to the hospital and…"

"It will do," I said. "A face-lift would certainly help, but the food is excellent."

"Ha! Very good."

Dr. Phelps stopped outside the exam room.

"And to think you could have owned that place," he said, pulling a pair of latex gloves from a box affixed to the wall just outside the door.

"*I* could have?" I asked, stunned.

"Your father was negotiating a deal to purchase the property just before he passed. The deal was never finalized, and it was passed on to you to decide what to do with it."

I cast my mind back. "I vaguely recall," I said, rubbing at the back of my neck. "Now that I think of it, the deal was with Mrs. Cuttleberry." The hotel owner's unsettling expression flashed across my mind.

"That's right," said Dr. Phelps. "You probably would have maintained the place better than she ever could."

I straightened. "Actually, I *do* remember. She wanted to sell, but I canceled the contract. I didn't even consider it very closely. I was too emotionally drained to pursue *any* business after having just lost my father. I canceled the deal and flew back to the States."

"Perfectly understandable. Besides, it's no matter now," he said, shrugging as he entered the exam room.

"So I've been told," I replied.

The following couple of weeks were fairly uneventful. My colleagues and I spent much of our time acclimating ourselves to our new venture—and successfully so. The patients seemed pleased with the additional medical care, and personally, I felt pleased with our contributions.

Having earned some time for rest and relaxation, Dr. Layton, Dr. Pruit, and I decided to retreat to the hotel's small courtyard. Slumped comfortably in a hammock nestled between two mango trees, I listened with amusement to my slightly inebriated colleague.

"These past two weeks," started Dr. Layton, raising his glass, "have been the *best* two weeks I've spent practicing medicine!" He brushed his dark hair from his forehead, the bright miniature umbrella in his glass sliding dangerously close to toppling out of his glass. His face was flushed. "I confess, Harrington, I fell for the seduction of those sandy beaches and beautiful ocean waves, and it was then that I knew I had to stay!"

"Not to mention the patients we've helped, Rick," remarked Dr. Pruit in good humor.

"Oh right! Of course, Wendy!"

Wendy's husky laugh echoed alongside the sound of the waves crashing against the nearby cliffs.

"Of course! Of course!" reiterated my colleague. "To helping the patients!"

Dr. Layton lifted his glass again, and the miniature umbrella finally tumbled to the deck floor.

"Dr. Finch?" a voice whispered behind me.

Startled, I hastily steadied my hammock as I turned to find Mrs. Cuttleberry standing quietly in the doorway.

"Mrs. Cuttleberry, were we too loud?" I asked. I glanced at my watch.

"No, not at all. A package arrived for you earlier today."

She handed me the small parcel, which had no return address.

"Do you know who sent this?" I asked, lifting my eyes, but Mrs. Cuttleberry had already gone.

I opened the package to reveal a slice of fruit cake and a brief note.

"'Welcome back, Dr. Finch,'" I read aloud. "'Here is a small token of thanks for all you've done.'"

"Mmm, what's that?" asked Wendy, stepping beside me.

"A piece of fruit cake, but I'm not sure who sent it," I replied, handing Wendy the note.

"Looks like it's from the hospital," she decided, wafting the scent of the cake toward her nose. "Looks moist…and tasty." She grinned.

"Are you lobbying for a piece, Wendy?"

"I am."

"Then I insist you have it all. I've never been fond of fruit cake—it has too strong a flavor for me."

"*Really?*" she said, breaking the thick, dark cake between

her fingers. "Growing up here, I would have thought you'd love the stuff!"

"One would think so. But listen," I said as I rolled out of the hammock, "you guys enjoy yourselves. I need to get some rest."

Wishing my colleagues a good night, I walked back into the hotel and down the dimly lit hallway toward my room. I'd only been in my room a short time when I heard footsteps rushing down the hall. Curious, I peeked out my door and discovered Dr. Layton running toward me.

"Harrington!" Dr. Layton's face was pale and dotted with sweat. "Convulsions!" he yelled. "She just went into convulsions! I... I..."

"*Who* has gone into convulsions, Rick?" I demanded, gripping his shoulders.

"Wendy!" Dr. Layton grasped the sides of his head. "It's Wendy!"

"Then *come on!*" I yelled, rushing past him, but Dr. Layton didn't follow.

"Harrington!" Dr. Layton called behind me. "Wendy is *dead!*"

My step faltered, and I staggered against the wall.

"That can't be!" I exclaimed. "I was just talking to her!" I peered at my colleague's solemn face.

"Mrs. Cuttleberry is on the phone with the police right now," he replied.

"I was *just* talking to her!" I repeated as Dr. Layton shook his head, and I was certain that he would not have made a mistake in his diagnosis.

"Wendy is dead," he murmured.

∽

Confusion muddled my mind, and I found myself taking a long walk early the following morning. Nostalgia led me to my old high school, Rusea's High School, a massive brick structure situated at the top of a cliff.

I breathed in deeply as I looked out to the ocean, wondering how in the world things had gone so terribly wrong. Wendy was dead, and the police had limited resources. Although samples of the fruit cake had been sent to Kingston for testing, it would still take time before we received the results. To add to my frustration, the locals had declared Wendy's death to be the result of witchcraft! Only in a small, rural town would anyone even utter such a word!

I cast my eyes toward the ocean again.

Murder, that's what this was. There had clearly been poison in the cake—the cake that was sent to me, but it was Wendy who had collapsed into convulsions. I rubbed slowly at my temples.

"Boss man!"

I spun around, the gravel beneath my feet tumbling over the edge of the cliff as I faced a man with a long shovel gripped in his hand.

"You all right, mon?" he called as he approached.

"Yes," I lied, nodding my head. "I was just out for a walk."

"You're the doctor, mon?"

"That's right," I replied cautiously, walking toward him.

"I recognize you from the hospital," he continued. "The name is Joseph Durant, but people call me Jo Jo."

Jo Jo's grip on his shovel loosened, allowing the tip of the spade to bury itself in the gravel. Realizing that I didn't recognize him, he added, "I had the bad shoulder," and tapped a pair of calloused fingers against his arm.

"I remember now," I replied. "Was Dr. Phelps able to help you?"

The man flashed a broad smile. "As always! Not the first coconut tree to do me harm." He studied me for a moment. "But what ya doing 'round here, mon?"

"I used to attend this high school," I remarked. I looked over at the old brick building before turning back to Jo Jo. "Just thought I'd come here to think."

Jo Jo tugged at the strap of his shabby overalls. "Sorry about your friend. I heard she died last night—at Tamarind Lodge."

I simply nodded my thanks. I couldn't say that I was surprised that he had already heard the tragic news.

"Well, it was nice running into you," I remarked faintly as I walked past Jo Jo, back toward the road I had come along.

"Yea, mon...but you ought to know..."

Jo Jo seemed to hesitate before saying something else, but I didn't wait to hear what that might have been. I was deeply lost in my own thoughts. I walked across the gravel onto the winding, concrete road, looking toward the church at the bottom of the small hill. It had been many years since I was there last.

"Boss man!"

I vaguely heard Jo Jo's call as I remained focused on the church. It was a beautiful church. I recalled the pipe organs booming through its walls, and the shiny wooden pews. Perhaps we could hold a service for Wendy. Yes, a service would be nice.

"*Boss man!*"

This time, the voice seemed thunderous. I turned around to find Jo Jo breathless, having sprinted to catch up with me.

"You need to leave that hotel, mon!" he yelled, slowing his stride as he fell into step beside me.

"Excuse me?" I felt heat rise in my cheeks. "What's all this about?"

"That hotel," he started again. "Obeah, mon—witchcraft. It's haunted. You've got to leave."

"*Haunted?*" I inhaled to calm myself. "My friend was *murdered*, Jo Jo, and to be frank, I don't have the energy or the patience to entertain the idea that witchcraft had to do with her death."

I turned my back without waiting for a reply and headed toward the bottom of the hill. I felt somewhat guilty as I knew that I had been far too terse with Jo Jo.

"There were more, you know!" he yelled behind me. "Your friend isn't the only one who's died there!"

I stopped and glared at Jo Jo over my shoulder, and he looked appealingly toward me.

"There have been others," he repeated.

I walked back up the path, my attention no longer divided.

"Tell me, Jo Jo," I said.

"It was ten years ago," he began as he rubbed the palm of his hand gingerly against his shoulder. "Mrs. Cuttleberry was married, but the man was no good. Whole town knew it. Too much drinking, mon. Always a glass in his hand. So Mrs. Cuttleberry decided to leave him. She made plans to sell her lodge and leave, but something happened." Jo Jo's brows drew together as he attempted to recall until, finally, he shook his head. "No, I don't know all the details, but no one bought the property. She ended up having to stay."

I winced as my father's business deal from ten years ago immediately rushed to mind—the contract *I* had canceled.

"Mr. Cuttleberry only got worse once he found out what his wife was up to, wanting to sell and move away," Jo Jo continued.

"And we all knew those bruises on her face weren't from tripping down any stairs. Then one night, it was *Mr.* Cuttleberry who tripped down the stairs, but he didn't just come out of it with bruises, you understand?"

I nodded.

"Police saw that he had been drunk and ruled it an accidental death." Jo Jo shrugged. "Whether it was accidental or not made no difference to us, mon, but it was the second death that had us nervous."

"A second death?" I asked.

"Yea, mon!" Jo Jo lowered his voice. "It was a guest that was staying at the lodge during the time that Mr. Cuttleberry died. His room was just at the bottom of the stairs where they found Mr. Cuttleberry's body. They knocked on his door to question him, but there he was—dead! Food poisoning, they said, since he had a tray of food half eaten in his room. Illness took him over, they said."

Jo Jo shook his head.

"It was Mr. Cuttleberry come back to haunt the place! You tell me how just after that man dies, another dies right near where his body was found? Mr. Cuttleberry come *back*, mon!"

"That's nonsense, Jo Jo!" I exclaimed.

Slowly, Jo Jo lifted his shovel and pointed the worn, soiled handle toward my chest.

"There was no blood. Just dead bodies—and all at Tamarind Lodge. And now your friend. No blood. Just gone, passed on. Mark my words, boss man, it's Obeah. Stay away from that place!"

With that, Jo Jo took his shovel and left.

❦

Within the hour, I entered Dr. Phelps's office and found him in distress.

"What's happened?" I asked, my voice surprisingly hoarse.

"Wendy's blood sample…"

"Yes?"

Dr. Phelps cleared his throat. "I made sure to draw the blood myself, and on my first venipuncture"—he looked at me knowingly—"bright-red venous blood filled the syringe."

"Cyanide," I uttered.

I drew my hand across my face, taking in a jagged breath.

"It wasn't meant for Wendy," I exclaimed. My face twisted as a wave of repulsion washed over me. I turned toward the doctor. "Someone intended that *I* would die of cyanide. The cake that Wendy ate was meant for me."

"But why?" demanded Dr. Phelps, bursting from his seat.

I shook my head. "I…I have no idea. I knew that what happened to Wendy was probably intended for me, but now that you've confirmed that it really was poison—"

Dr. Phelps slapped the palm of his hand against the desk, startling me to attention.

"Who would want you dead, Harrington?"

"What an insane question!" I exclaimed.

"And yet we *have* to ask it! Wendy is *dead*, and you were the intended victim. Think!"

Urging my mind to provide answers, I paced the small office. Someone wanted to kill me in a place where I hadn't been for ten years. *Ten* years!

I closed my eyes, negotiating with my nerves. It all seemed so ridiculous, and yet it was happening. I stilled as my mind systematically recalled every conversation, every detail, since my arrival. Warily, I turned toward Dr. Phelps.

"Dr. Phelps," I began, leaning the weight of my body against his desk, "the *only* person that I can possibly imagine having anything against me is Mrs. Cuttleberry. I've only recently learned that ten years ago I denied her the sale of Tamarind Lodge, at a time when she needed it most, and now I've walked right back into the place!"

"Mrs. Cuttleberry?" replied Dr. Phelps, his expression doubtful. "I can't imagine that such a benign woma—"

"Jo Jo told me about her abusive husband and his 'accidental' death, Dr. Phelps. And then another man died soon after. You tell me that's not the least bit strange. And you tell me that she wouldn't bear me a grudge for canceling what she had counted on so desperately from my father." I took a deep breath and wiped the back of my hand across my forehead. "Who knows how different her life would have been if I hadn't stopped the deal from going through. She would have had more than enough money to start a new life elsewhere. Instead, she has struggled all her life to keep up Tamarind Lodge—a prisoner to the very place she owns."

Dr. Phelps, his arms crossed, considered my ideas silently. I waited, pacing, watching as he stroked his chin and mulled over the plausibility of what I had suggested. Had Wendy's death not been proof of the danger I was in, I wouldn't have believed any of it either!

"I think you may have something," he finally replied. "Resentment can be a chronic condition, festering in one's soul if left untreated."

Spoken, I thought, like a true doctor.

"Yes." He nodded again. "I think you may have something." Dr. Phelps peered at me over the top of his glasses. "Are you willing to pay Mrs. Cuttleberry a visit?"

"I am," I replied, opening the office door.

"Nurse Peckleton!" called Dr. Phelps as we strode hurriedly past the nurse's station. "Dr. Finch and I won't be available for at least the next couple of hours. If there is an emergency, you can find us at Tamarind Lodge. We need to meet with Mrs. Cuttleberry."

"Mrs. Cuttleberry?" said Ms. Peckleton, running after us. "But, Dr. Phelps," she said, her expression uncertain, "haven't you heard? Mrs. Cuttleberry was just admitted to intensive care. Dr. Layton is in with her now. She's been poisoned!"

⁓

With Mrs. Cuttleberry poisoned, I found myself completely confused. I didn't know what to make of all that was happening. I headed back to the Hanover Parish Church to think; it was a place I had always been fond of since I was a young boy.

I cast my eyes over the beautifully blemished tombstones that had inhabited the churchyard for decades. They seemed eerily appropriate as I considered past deaths, yet now I considered death of a more heinous nature. Kicking the loose gravel with my shoe, I stepped beneath a majestic tree. Its branches cascaded over me, yet the sun, determined to reach me, streamed easily between its leaves.

"If not Mrs. Cuttleberry," I said aloud, "then who?"

"Good question," answered a familiar voice.

I lifted my eyes to find Dr. Layton approaching.

"Dr. Phelps said I would find you here," he remarked. "Just thought you should know that Mrs. Cuttleberry is stable. Maybe we should notify her family."

"I can't imagine that she has much family left," I said. "Her husband died years ago."

"What about her child?" asked Dr. Layton.

I leaned back against the tree's sturdy trunk. "I can't imagine Mrs. Cuttleberry having any children, can you?"

A faint smile tugged at Dr. Layton's lips.

"I wouldn't have believed it either," he admitted, "if it weren't for her scar. I noted it during her exam. Mrs. Cuttleberry has had a C-section. She has had at least one child…"

I straightened, pulling myself from the tree. "A *child*…"

Dr. Layton frowned. "Is that significant?"

I turned at the sound of leaves crunching under someone's feet.

"You all right, gentlemen?"

An older, square-faced man dressed in a black, short-sleeve button-down shirt with a white band around his collar approached. His smile was welcoming.

"Reverend!" I called, striding toward him. "Sir, you've served at this parish church for several years, correct?"

"Yes," he confirmed, slowing his own steps as I moved excitedly toward him. "Almost forty years."

"Then you would be familiar with any children born here?"

"That's right…" The reverend's eyes peered questioningly past me toward Dr. Layton.

"I apologize for my abruptness," I said, "but could you please tell me…do you remember if Mrs. Cuttleberry had a child?"

"Mrs. Cuttleberry from Tamarind Lodge?" he asked, the pitch of his voice rising.

"Yes, exactly."

"Well…yes," he answered. "I remember quite well. She had a daughter, Rosalind."

"Ms. Rosalind Cuttleberry," I reiterated. "Rosalind?" I asked, directing my question to Dr. Layton.

Dr. Layton shook his head. He didn't know anyone by that name either.

"No, no," said the reverend. "Not Rosalind *Cuttleberry*. Mrs. Cuttleberry's child was from her *first* marriage to Mr. Avery Peckleton. She didn't marry Mr. Cuttleberry until years later."

"*Peckleton*," I uttered. "*Nurse* Rosalind Peckleton." I spun around. "Come on, Rick," I called. "We've got to get back to the hospital."

"I don't understand," replied Dr. Layton, breathing rapidly as he tried to keep up with me. "What does it matter that Nurse Peckleton is Mrs. Cuttleberry's daughter?"

"It means that ten years ago it wasn't just Mrs. Cuttleberry who didn't benefit from the sale of the hotel, and it wasn't just Mrs. Cuttleberry who was under the tyranny of an abusive husband. Nurse Peckleton was also there. And she went through everything Mrs. Cuttleberry did."

Dr. Layton grabbed me by my shoulder. "Do you mean Nurse Peckleton poisoned Wendy, but she actually meant to kill you, for revenge?"

"Yes. Just as she is responsible for the other murders at Tamarind Lodge ten years ago."

❧

Dr. Layton and I arrived at the hospital in record time, and my colleague agreed to treat the waiting patients as Dr. Phelps and I went to confront Nurse Peckleton.

We reached Mrs. Cuttleberry's room and found Nurse Peckleton sitting at her bedside. Her eyes narrowed when she saw us enter.

"Dr. Finch? Dr. Phelps?" she began.

I looked toward Mrs. Cuttleberry, who lay motionless on the bed.

"Visiting Mrs. Cuttleberry?" I asked.

"As a matter of fact, I am," replied Nurse Peckleton thoughtfully. "I care a great deal for my patients, Dr. Finch," she added, smiling. The arrogance behind her smile was obvious now.

"I'm sure," I replied. "Especially if they're family."

Nurse Peckleton's lips creased into a straight line. She looked toward Dr. Phelps.

"A mother's love is something special, isn't it?" I asked, drawing her eyes back to my own.

Clearing her throat, Ms. Peckleton stood and stepped toward us from the bed.

"So, you know?" she uttered, her voice husky.

"You resented me because I cost you your freedom," I said.

Nurse Peckleton nodded her head slowly.

"You understand," she replied wearily, looking between Dr. Phelps and me. "It was unfortunate that your father passed before the sale of Tamarind Lodge was complete, Dr. Finch. We would have had enough money to move away from that abusive man—my mother and I." She drew in slow, steady breaths. "But you canceled the contract and left...just *left*, Dr. Finch."

She glared at me, studying me closely.

"You could leave," she said. "*You* could do whatever you wanted, and the contract that mattered so much to us meant *nothing* to you. Her hands trembled as she raised them to her chest. "But we were still here with that drunken man and no means of escape. So, yes, as I am sure you are aware, his death was no accident. I killed my stepfather."

Her voice was eerily calm, as though she was not recalling how she had murdered a man. Ms. Peckleton stepped back, lowering herself slowly onto the bed beside her mother.

"I pushed him down the stairs," she went on. "People believed it was an accident—he was known to enjoy his drink. But then"—she frowned—"there was that man at the foot of the stairs."

She looked directly at me.

"He was a guest at the hotel. He heard the noise of the fall—my stepfather's drunk, limp body tumbling down—and he came out of his room. He saw me..." Ms. Peckleton silently debated with herself for a moment and then shook her head. "No, I don't recall his name, but I had to get rid of him."

She peered at Dr. Phelps with sudden amusement in her eyes.

"Locals have said the place is haunted—cursed, even—ever since the death of my stepfather!" She laughed. "I went along with that idea because no one talked of murder. No." She shook her head. "Witchcraft, Mr. Cuttleberry's ghost, but not *murder*!"

"And what of your missing father?" I demanded. "Mr. Avery Peckleton. Was that just something you made up to perpetuate the myth of the haunted hotel?"

Mrs. Peckleton grew rigid.

"Oh yes...father dear," she began, breathing in deeply. Her eyes darted upward. "No, he wasn't technically *missing*," she said, turning her gaze back upon me. "Do you know he came to the hotel to see me? He figured it out—what I had done."

Nurse Peckleton looked toward her mother as she continued.

"I suspect that Mother always knew I had something to do

with it, but she never asked. Besides, she never loved me any less…"

Nurse Peckleton lifted her eyes.

"I think Mother must have shared her concerns with my father, but he used what he learned to try to get money from me for his silence. *Money!* He wanted to take the little I had from me—his own daughter! I didn't have to *pay* for his silence when I could get it my own way," she sneered. "By then, I had learned quite a bit about poisons through my education in nursing. I poisoned him and hid the body—and *yes*, I told people he had gone missing to help my cause, to encourage the haunted hotel stories."

"I…I can't believe this," muttered Dr. Phelps.

"I'm sorry, Dr. Phelps," said Nurse Peckleton. Surprisingly, her tone seemed sincere. Again, she gazed tenderly at her mother. "Everything was finally behind me, behind us…but then Dr. Finch arrived, and everything came rushing back as though it had only happened yesterday."

"You were at Tamarind Lodge the night I arrived," I recalled aloud, remembering the shadow that had moved swiftly across the hall just behind Mrs. Cuttleberry. "I wondered who it was at the time, but now it makes sense—it must have been you who was there that night."

An impish grin formed on Ms. Peckleton's face.

"Yes, I was there," she admitted. "I had to leave before you saw me. I knew from the reservation that you were coming, and when I finally saw you, I…I snapped. I couldn't take it. It was because of *you*," she said. "Don't you see that *you* are the reason I did all this?"

"Then why poison your own mother?" interjected Dr. Phelps. "If you supposedly care so much for her."

Nurse Peckleton remained eerily calm.

"I knew you would consider my mother a suspect," she replied. "I had to do something that would prove she wasn't involved. I gave her arsenic—only enough to make her ill, not enough to kill her."

"You do realize it's over, Ms. Peckleton?" asked Dr. Phelps. "This is it. It's all over…"

Nurse Peckleton nodded.

"I do," she replied, shrugging. "It's no matter now."

HUGO FLYNN MYSTERIES

ORIGINALLY WRITTEN FOR THE *SHERLOCK HOLMES MYSTERY MAGAZINE*

(USA PUBLICATION)

FOUR
WHY DIE TWICE?

A NEW CHAPTER in my life began, as many often do, quite abruptly and just after a significant loss in my life. In my case, it was the loss of my employment at the *Times*, and I found myself one Friday evening in the city of Linbank. It was here that I forced my way through a rather dry, feeble sandwich, courtesy of a small deli into which I had aimlessly wandered. As I think back now, I can honestly say that I had little idea of how drastically my life would change due to the few events that followed.

There was rain, of course, on what was already a miserable evening, and with little idea of where I intended to go, I simply rushed out of the small sandwich shop and headed in the general direction of a strip of brick buildings, each with its own concrete stoop falling neatly in line with the next. It was just as I passed the first of these that I inadvertently collided with a tall, slender man in an expensive suit.

"David!" he said, extending his hand. "If it isn't David Merrick—it's been quite a while!"

Very much to my surprise, the man knew me, and it was only as the haze of what had been a horrible day cleared that I realized I knew him as well.

"Hugo Flynn!" I declared.

He was my college roommate from years ago.

Pulling up the collar of my jacket, I asked, "How have you been?"

"Fine, fine," he replied as it began to rain more heavily. "I'm in this building, just a few feet away."

He pointed at a building named Haughton Court. I nodded as I followed behind him.

Hugo was much improved in his appearance, and I understood in that moment why he had not been so readily recognizable to me.

It had been several years—at least ten—since I had seen him last, and back then, he had had a strong, jutting chin and an equally, I'm afraid to say, large forehead. It was the type of prominent forehead that suggested that what he might lack in classically handsome features, he made up for in unquestionable intellect. Today, however, he had a stylish mess of dark, wavy brown hair that fell loosely over this…impressive attribute. As a matter of fact, as I would come to discover later, his forehead was now only ever fully exposed when he was perplexed, as it was only then that he would absently brush his hand through his hair and away from his face.

"I'm lucky I ran into you," I started as Hugo placed a steaming pot of coffee beside me. "I would have been soaked before I reached the end of Tremson Street."

Without replying, Hugo hurriedly collected some scattered music sheets from an antique wing chair and piled them onto the bench of a baby grand piano in the corner of his luxurious loft space.

"Hmm," he mumbled. "I probably should offer you snacks or something to eat—crackers, little cubes of cheese with toothpicks in them…" He peered at me through his square-shaped frames apologetically. "Mrs. Bradley, my housekeeper, is off for the evening." He shrugged. "She tends to take care of these particulars, and I'm a bit useless at some things…but maybe I could make—"

Hugo's voice suddenly broke off. In response to the sober change in his expression, I spun around just as the front door swung open and crashed against the wall. Standing in the doorway was a heavy-set man of about average height. His jaw was clenched, emphasizing the square shape of his face, and his dark hair, which was wet from the rain, clung to his temples. As he stumbled inside, water dripped onto the hardwood floor with each step, leaving vague outlines of the tattered soles of his work boots.

The man peered with wide eyes directly into mine.

"Are you Mr. Flynn?" he asked. His chest rose as though he was finding it difficult to speak.

"*I* am Mr. Flynn," stated Hugo as he stepped forward, blocking me from direct view.

I peered over Hugo's shoulder as the man's eyes settled on my friend.

"A crime…" he said.

I am embarrassed to say that my journalist instincts immediately resurfaced, and I interjected shamefully. "What's that? Is there a crime that's just happened? Near here?"

The man shifted his eyes back toward mine, his expression puzzled.

"No." He inhaled another jagged breath before continuing. "Yesterday… It was *yesterday*, Mr. Flynn, that I was murdered."

Then quite suddenly, like a scene from a horror movie, the man's face contorted and he fell into convulsions on the floor! It was only a matter of seconds before he suddenly stopped moving. He was dead. *Dead.*

I think I muttered various exclamations under my breath, but to be truthful, I can't recall what they might have been. I do remember, however, looking appealingly toward Hugo with my mouth hanging open, expecting to see a similarly shocked expression on the face of my friend. What a comfort that would have been, to have someone to whom I could relate during such an awful experience!

Instead, Hugo was standing poised, in a relaxed manner, with a hand on one hip and his other hand resting inquisitively on his chin.

Perhaps he felt the weight of my stare, because he suddenly seemed to be both aware of and startled by my presence. He looked from the body to me, then to the steaming pot of coffee, then back to the body once more. He opened his mouth as if to say something and then closed it again indecisively. I encouraged him to say something—*anything*—in regard to what had just happened.

Finally, he remarked, "Well, would it be…I mean, I'm not very good at some things…knowing when to get cheese and crackers and whatnot." He shifted his weight, glancing once more from the body to the pot of coffee and then back to me. "Would you consider it extremely rude of me if I didn't…" Hugo pressed his lips together, then started again. "The coffee, with you, I mean…and instead…if I tended to this…"

He waved his slender hand over the body.

"This...*situation*?"

He had finished at last. I didn't immediately reply, for I was both astonished and suddenly reminded of my old friend from so long ago. Hugo was a man of impressive intellect, yet he had always been incredibly uneasy in the most typical, everyday social settings. An *extraordinary* man in complicated matters, but he would overanalyze the simplest of concepts!

"*Please* do!" I yelled. "Forget about sharing coffee with me!"

Jumping slightly at my starkness, Hugo nodded appreciatively and knelt over the man's body. It was in this moment that I wondered what had become of Hugo Flynn. Why was it that a dead body was not alarming to the man? I asked him as much.

Hugo paused, holding the dead man's arm a foot above the floor, his stiff wrist pinched between Hugo's fingertips.

"What do I do?" he repeated, his hair shifting on his forehead as his eyebrows rose. "Oh, of course. I can see why you'd probably want to know—people bursting into apartments and keeling over and whatnot, yes."

Standing, Hugo pulled out a card and handed it to me.

"I'm a private investigator. Have my own business. People come to me for help."

"Or to die?" I questioned, directing my gaze toward the floor.

Hugo tilted his head to one side as he considered the body.

"Excellent point, David. They don't typically die *here*..." He mulled over the idea while cleaning the lenses of his glasses. Replacing them on his face, he added reminiscently, "*Although*, there was that incident with the podiatrist, but that was more of a *near*-death experience...just saved her in time. Poison—the whole thing was..." He shook his head disagreeably. "I've never been fond of feet, but even less since."

I just stared at Hugo but said nothing. I really didn't know what to say.

Turning, Hugo paced the living area before eventually resting his elbow on the mantel above the fireplace. He refocused on the body.

"They usually stay there, don't they?" he asked aloud, considering my point further. "Where they've been murdered, I mean."

"I would think so," I replied under my breath.

Pulling latex gloves from his pocket, he strode across the room.

"And *yesterday*, apparently," he mumbled. "He was murdered *yesterday*?" Hugo frowned. "What a remarkable thing to say."

Crouching beside the body, Hugo worked his way around the man while on all fours, sniffing the air like some sort of hound dog and examining the body in a manner that I could only presume was effective when hunting for clues.

"The smell of bitter almonds," he muttered. "Cyanide."

Studying the man's face, Hugo seemed to take a special interest in the skin behind the man's ear.

"Is there something there?" I asked.

"A scar. It starts from the back of the ear and extends down his neck and toward his collarbone." Turning his gaze toward me, he added, "Doesn't look recent. I doubt it has to do with his death."

Hesitantly, I stepped forward and nodded in agreement.

Patting down the man's damp clothes, Hugo beamed with interest as he pulled a folded newspaper clipping from the jacket pocket. Carefully, he placed the soaked paper onto his coffee table, his tall figure hunched forward—the very image of a mad scientist at work in his lab.

Anxiously, I watched as he carefully unfolded the article and dabbed it dry with his handkerchief. I couldn't help but wonder if he should be tampering with police evidence. After all, how much liberty does a private investigator really have?

"Shouldn't we call the police?" I blurted out.

"Police?" Hugo looked at me in disbelief. "Yes, of course!" he exclaimed. "This man is *dead*!" He looked dumbfounded that I had even asked.

"Right, how silly of me," I mumbled as Hugo returned to his task.

It was only a matter of minutes before he straightened, a broad smile sweeping across his face.

"It's clear enough now, I think," he said, referring to the newspaper article.

I must admit, my interest was piqued, and I looked over the damp page that clung to the glass tabletop. My eye separated out the faint text that seeped through from the other side as I read the headline.

"MAN FOUND DEAD IN DOVER," it stated. The article went on to say:

Thursday night, the body of Dover Hills resident Gordon Saddler was found in his home. Police baffled as to possible motive, citing that "no items appear to have been stolen from his residence." Saddler was a respected, well-liked member of the small town, and he will be greatly missed. Saddler leaves behind no known relatives.

"I've got to head to Dover Hills," declared Hugo. Frowning, he added, "I still owe you coffee..."

"No, please. It's really not a big deal," I replied.

"Are you okay with murders and things?" he asked.

Not knowing exactly how best to answer that question, nor entirely sure as to what "things" he was referring to, my reply was guarded.

"I was a journalist in Afghanistan for a while. Saw some *things* that weren't easy to witness."

"Then how about a cup of coffee in Dover?" he asked. "Just know there will be talk of murder."

I glanced at the body mere feet away, debating silently.

"As a matter of fact," I finally answered, "my availability has recently opened up."

"Good."

I briefly pondered whether I was making a wise decision in pursuing further interest in this shocking death, but to be honest, I was curious, and what else had I really to do? It was on this flimsy reasoning that the new chapter of my life began.

The police arrived and took our statements. Hugo clearly had an established relationship with many of the officers, including Lead Detective Sophia Shaw—a competent woman with long, dark, wavy hair and striking dark-brown eyes. I immediately took a liking to her. Admittedly, my interest may have reached a bit beyond professional principles, but I was disappointed to find that she only paid me a cursory glance. I am but a man of average height with short blond hair, an athletic build, and a slightly crooked nose from an old football injury, but attractive overall, I think. However, it appeared to me that Detective Shaw was a woman of an intensely single-minded focus, and rightfully so when investigating a murder.

"I will give you a call when I've confirmed the cause of death and identified our John Doe," she stated to Hugo in a direct manner. "I expect you're heading to Dover?"

"I am," replied Hugo.

"I will give them a call, let them know what to expect."

A tiny smile peeked through the lead detective's otherwise serious expression, and I found myself irrationally jealous of the relationship Hugo had established with Detective Shaw. Hugo seemed not to notice, of course, and redirected his attention once more to the dead body.

While Hugo absentmindedly brushed his hair back from his forehead, Detective Shaw took her leave, and the forensics team finished working the scene.

"We'll leave at eight tomorrow morning.?" asked Hugo once everyone had finally gone from the apartment.

"That would be fine," I agreed. "I'm looking forward to it."

To be honest, I genuinely was.

⁓

It was first thing in the morning when Hugo and I headed to Dover Hills. It took just over an hour's drive to reach the town, and the newspaper had been quite accurate in classifying it as "small." It held an old-world charm in its brick buildings and its abundance of colorful flowers on windowsills. I glimpsed a single post office in which I strongly suspected locals would be greeted by name upon entering. I was not surprised, therefore, that we garnered several curious stares from the residents we passed on the street, particularly those who observed us pull into the Dover Hills police station.

It was obvious upon entering that the police station was an older building, but the sunlight that streamed in through the large windows brightened the drab furniture and linoleum flooring. It also, however, made the space uncomfortably warm.

"Please, have a seat," offered Sergeant Kinley.

Sergeant Kinley's expression was stern as we took a seat in front of his desk. He crossed his brawny arms over his gray uniform shirt and black tie that rested askew across his chest, dipping and then rising with the curve of his stout belly. With the exception of his thinning hair that fluttered in response to a small fan hanging in the corner of the office, Sergeant Kinley remained motionless. Was he debating something? Was he trying to unnerve us? I couldn't be sure, but Hugo seemed unaffected.

Finally, the sergeant remarked, "We don't typically work with private eyes, Mr."—he glanced at a note on his desk—"Hugo Flynn."

Reclining in his chair, he grew silent again. Just the faint buzzing from the fan filled the stuffy space. He cast a critical eye over Hugo and then went on.

"But then again, we also don't get many murders around here." He scratched at the stubble on his chin. "I received a call from Detective Shaw recommending that I hear you out. You've got some experience in these matters, it seems."

"I do," replied Hugo.

"Of course," continued the sergeant, "I explained to her that my men and I have the case under control—it is, after all, in our town, our jurisdiction." He gave us a cautionary glance and cleared his throat. "Still, I am never opposed to the input of others, and if this might help you with your case—"

"Yes, we think it would really help us with our case," I interjected, feeling as though I could contribute in at least a small way. (I strongly suspected that diplomacy was not one of Hugo's strengths.)

The sergeant gave a single nod and opened a folder he had already laid out on his desk.

"Let me just go ahead and tell you what we've got," he started, his chair squeaking as he leaned forward. "A fellow by the name of Gordon Saddler was murdered Thursday night. Decent fellow. Pretty quiet, but personable. We couldn't find a motive. Nothing was stolen from his house, and no one can think of any possible enemies."

"And how long had he lived here?" asked Hugo.

"I'd say a little over a year. Inherited Old Man Jones's house—an uncle who was fond of him."

"How was he murdered?" I asked.

"Shot...and up close." The inspector tapped his temple. "It seemed pretty vindictive, if you ask me. Personal."

Hugo nodded. "Do you mind showing us Mr. Saddler's residence?"

"No, not at all."

I was relieved when we could leave the station and get out into the fresh air again. We followed behind Sergeant Kinley, but the drive wasn't far. In fact, we could have walked. In a way, I wish we had. Upon entering Saddler's house, I was accosted by the heavy smell of cigarettes, and once again, I yearned for the fresh air of the outdoors.

Inside Saddler's house, there was nothing of extraordinary significance that I could see. The door had been forced in the middle of the night, but that was hardly surprising considering the flimsy lock.

"It's a small town," replied the inspector when he noticed my expression as I examined the damaged keyhole. "Most people don't feel the need for high-end security here."

Hugo seemed somewhat quiet as we inspected the house. I asked him if anything seemed to stand out to him, and he replied that it didn't.

"Is this the room in which the murder took place?" asked Hugo as we entered the living area.

"Yes, right over there." Sergeant Kinley pointed toward the fireplace.

"Did you see anything unusual when you arrived on the scene?" I asked.

"Not a thing," he answered. "The TV was left on, but I wouldn't consider that odd."

I crossed between two faded green couches and knelt beside Hugo, who was examining the fireplace.

"The fireplace doesn't look like it has been used in a while," he remarked. "And there is a bit of blood still on the floor..."

"There are also some cigarettes scattered over here," I noted. "About a foot away from the blood."

Standing, Hugo examined the mantelpiece and found a near-empty cigarette packet lying on its side. A few cigarettes remained, partially sticking out of the casing.

"So, let's imagine that Saddler was seated on his couch," started Hugo. "He decides he wants a cigarette, walks to the mantelpiece, and our intruder surprises him from behind. The intruder shoots him, causing the box to overturn and the cigarettes to scatter across the floor."

"Then Saddler," I continued, "falls to the ground, leaving the remains of blood on the floor near the fireplace."

"Pretty simple," replied Hugo. "It seems as though he was

simply having a relaxing evening in, watching television. It doesn't seem like the behavior of a man expecting someone to come after him."

Sergeant Kinley remarked, "He didn't seem the type to have any enemies."

"But he has only lived here a year," I countered. "He might have made enemies in his past who aren't from this town."

"That's always a possibility," conceded the sergeant.

Hugo dusted off his crisp black slacks.

"Nothing more to see in here," he decided. Turning toward the sergeant, he asked, "Did Mr. Saddler have any roommates? Any regular visitors?"

"No roommates," answered Sergeant Kinley as we followed him out of the house. "As far as visitors, only the gardener, Mr. Finkler—Elbert Finkler. He should be here any minute." Sergeant Kinley pulled Mr. Saddler's door shut as he added, "Mr. Finkler asked us if he could finish weeding Saddler's yard, seeing that he had been paid through the month and he was nearly done. We saw no problem with it. Good man, Finkler."

"He sounds like an honest man," I said.

"That he is," agreed the sergeant just before he received an announcement on his radio. He replied into the receiver. "I'm on my way." Looking between Hugo and me, he said, "Listen, I've got to tend to another call. Can I lead you back to the station or anywhere else?"

Hugo declined. "If it's all right with you, we'd like to wait for the gardener—ask him a few questions."

"Suit yourself. Just call me if you need anything."

Hugo and I took a seat on Saddler's front porch as we watched the sergeant's tires kick up the loose gravel on the road as he drove away. I took the opportunity to discuss the man who had died in Hugo's apartment.

"What I don't understand," I said, "is what our murdered man has to do with this Gordon Saddler fellow. Obviously, there is a connection or else he wouldn't have had the newspaper article."

Hugo agreed. "I expect we will have an answer to that question once we figure out his name. I'm sure Detective Shaw is working on that now."

Hugo suddenly stood, and I peered beyond him to see an older man with a burlap sack on his back walking up the road toward Mr. Saddler's house.

"Mr. Finkler?" called Hugo as the older man drew closer.

"That's right. I'm Elbert Finkler," he replied and extended a blemished hand, the skin dotted by years of hard work under the sun. "You boys must be those private detectives the whole town has been buzzing about."

His cheeks rose to meet the corners of his eyes as he smiled.

"And why do you think that, Mr. Finkler?" asked Hugo, amused.

"I know 'bout everyone here—most people should, shouldn't they? Can count us all on one hand."

Mr. Finkler chuckled.

"*All right*," he said. "You detectives are gonna figure it out. No use fibbin'." He raised both hands. "You can count us on two!"

Mr. Finkler wheezed, then laughed heartily to himself as he started once more toward Mr. Saddler's front yard.

"Also, not much need for those fancy suits 'round here, young man," he added over his shoulder. His eyes were attentive as he studied Hugo with some interest before swinging his sack off his back and onto the ground.

"Armerni or Armonti—something like that, isn't it? I've got a niece. Wants to be some sort of fashion designer. She lives in the big city. Tells me all 'bout it. I can see you boys are the big-city type."

"We are from the city," I confirmed. "And we are here to investigate the death of Mr. Gordon Saddler."

Mr. Finkler's tanned, wrinkled forehead scrunched up with interest. "I figured you might be," he said. "Saw you standin' on Saddler's doorstep and figured you must be here 'bout his murder." He shook his head sadly.

"You were fond of Mr. Saddler?" asked Hugo.

"Oh yes, very. Still can't believe what happened. Seems unreal."

"He took over this house from Mr. Jones Saddler, correct?" I asked.

"Sure did," confirmed Mr. Finkler. "Old Jones was pretty fond of Gordon. The only relation I've ever heard him speak of. Said he was a chip off the old block, but I disagree." He grunted.

"You didn't like Mr. Jones?" asked Hugo.

"Well, I don't like to be speakin' ill of the dead, but I thought Old Jones was a bit crooked. He hired me once to take care of his lawn for him, but then paid me fifty dollars less than he promised. Couldn't prove it, what we agreed on, so I took the money and left, but I know what we shook on. Never did do his lawn again. No, sir." Elbert Finkler stamped his foot on the ground. "*No*, sir," he added once more.

"At least you got along well with Mr. Saddler," I said.

"To be honest," he said, leaning a bit closer, "I was glad to find that Gordon Saddler wasn't much like Old Jones at all.

Respectable and even paid me extra when he was real pleased with my work." He lifted his chin. "That's why I wanted to finish out his weeding proper."

Mr. Finkler cast an inspecting eye over the yard.

"Good man, Gordon Saddler, and just last week he was even in the paper."

"Really?" asked Hugo. "What was the story about?"

"His helping our youth. We've got a small recreation center here in town, and we all celebrated him for fixin' it up so the kids could use it. Got his picture in the paper and everything."

"Do you have a copy of the paper?" asked Hugo.

Mr. Finkler shook his head. "Not on me, but you give me a minute, and I'll find one. You wait and see."

It was half past three when we headed back toward Linbank. I felt that we had made little progress, but Hugo seemed to think we had collected enough clues to start forming a picture of the murder. As I drove, I glanced periodically at Hugo, who busily studied the newspaper article featuring Gordon Saddler. It was nothing of interest, in my opinion. It simply reiterated what Mr. Finkler had already told us, and it featured an unoriginal photo of a smiling Saddler crouching down beside the kids of the recreation center. I'm not sure what interested him so, but he must have read the article in silence ten times over. It was when we received a call from Detective Shaw, however, that Hugo's pensive mood turned quite animated.

"Detective Shaw," greeted Hugo as I listened to his side of the conversation.

"No, I've never seen the man before... Oh! Criminal

background, you say?" He nudged me. "Involved with any of my other cases?" Hugo rubbed the back of his neck. "No. No, I'm positive he wasn't. I would have remembered. Did he have prison time?"

Hugo nodded.

"And how long did he serve?" Hugo rubbed at his chin thoughtfully as the detective spoke. "Oh, I see," he replied into the receiver. "That is interesting. And when was he released? Ah, then he probably came after him… Right, I think so too. Cyanide poisoning? As I figured. Okay, and what was the man's name?"

It was here that Hugo suddenly drew in a breath. I slowed the car to get a good look at him as he mouthed the name to me, but I couldn't make out what it was.

"Are you sure?" asked Hugo once more into the phone. "Right, of course. Thank you, Detective Shaw. I will call you as soon as I get more information from my end."

"What? What's happened, Hugo?" I asked excitedly.

"Our murdered man, the one who burst into my apartment, he served time…he'd been convicted of a whole list of crimes. Apparently, he was released over four years ago and dropped off the grid. No one has seen him since, but there was another man, Leo Grimes, who was double-crossed by him in his less-than-legal business dealings. He was just released from prison about two months ago."

"Oh, well, that sounds simple enough," I said as I turned Hugo's car onto Tremson Street. "Leo Grimes wants revenge, tracks down the man, and does him in. Cyanide? Like you mentioned before?"

"Right, but get this." Hugo turned to me as I pulled the car up to the curb by Haughton Court and cut the engine.

"The *name* of the man who died in my apartment is *Gordon Saddler*—he has the same name as the victim in Dover Hills."

I was taken aback. "Coincidence?" I asked feebly. "People do have the same names…"

Hugo tossed me the paper.

"I don't think so," he said. "Take a close look at the picture. What do you see?"

I studied it but found nothing extraordinary. I told him as much.

"Imagine our Dover Hills Saddler without the beard," he encouraged.

I did as instructed, and it was only after a few moments that I realized Hugo's point.

"Without the beard, he would look *exactly* like the man from your apartment!" I declared.

"*Exactly*, and apparently, *like the man from my apartment told us*, he was killed the day before we saw him die."

"'Yesterday I was murdered,'" I muttered, repeating the strange words of the man who had burst through Hugo's door on Friday evening before suddenly dying.

"So, Thursday night, Gordon Saddler is killed in Dover Hills," considered Hugo aloud, "but then on Friday evening, he stumbles through my door and dies in my apartment."

"How could that be?" I asked as we exited the car. "How can someone die twice?"

Hugo didn't reply. Deep in thought, he simply brushed his hair back from his forehead and climbed the steps to his apartment.

∽

Two days had gone by, and Hugo had spoken very little of the case and very little in general for that matter. I often found him in the corner of his loft playing a series of original compositions on his piano while deep in thought, and then quite suddenly, as if remembering I was there, he would apologize for his rudeness and endeavor to make "small talk"—quite unsuccessfully, of course.

"Useless at these types of things," he would inevitably mutter.

I assured him that I was fine, and having previously been his roommate, I was quite aware of his awkward social manner.

"I know your strengths"—I shrugged—"and small talk is certainly not one of them. Let's stick to talking murder and unraveling grisly plots."

Hugo readily agreed, and I could tell he felt immense relief at my understanding.

"Besides," I joked, "your housekeeper, Mrs. Bradley, keeps me company."

Mrs. Bradley was a woman in her sixties, who sported a pile of gray curls on the top of her head and seemed to have been with Hugo for quite some time. I realized she was responsible not only for keeping the lofty four-bedroom "apartment" tidy but also for providing Hugo the sustenance he needed to survive. Had it not been for her wrinkled, loving hand pulling him to the table to eat, he would probably have starved.

It was on such an occasion as this that Mrs. Bradley, wearing a pink apron that read, "This meal is seasoned with love," brought unexpected clarity to Hugo.

"Now, if you don't sit down and eat, young man, you will wither away," she told him. "And I just don't know what I would tell your mother."

"I'm not very hungry, Mrs. Bradley," replied Hugo from his piano.

"I didn't ask you if you were, now, did I, dear?" she replied sweetly, placing two bowls of homemade chicken soup on the table. "You too, Mr. Merrick, come along." Turning her attention back to Hugo, she added, "You know, I have a sister who was once heartbroken over some boy who broke up with her and she didn't eat for days. Withered away, she did." Nudging Hugo to the table, she added, "And *you* certainly can't afford to do that, dear. If you get any skinnier, you won't be able to hold up that colossal cranium of yours."

Patting him on the back, she waited until he took his first bite before leaving the room.

It was midway through the meal that Hugo unexpectedly dropped his spoon and burst out of his chair.

"Of course!" he yelled. "How could I have been so foolish? Mrs. Bradley! Mrs. Bradley!"

Mrs. Bradley shot out from one of the hallways and slid quickly across the hardwood floor in her pink bedroom slippers, the fabric of her floral cardigan fluttering behind her. To my utter astonishment, she was holding a handgun!

"*Where are they?*" she yelled.

I jumped from my seat and moved out of her line of fire. Apparently completely comfortable with the fact that Mrs. Bradley was armed, Hugo ignored the gun and smacked a big kiss on her forehead.

"No one to shoot at today, Mrs. Bradley! Just wanted to tell you thanks."

A bit startled, she replied, "I'm glad you like the soup, dear. I'll be sure to make it again." Lowering her weapon, she added, "You see what a little nourishment can do? Gives us energy and—"

"No, no, Mrs. Bradley," interrupted Hugo as he laughed. "You solved the case! What you said!"

Clasping his hands together, Hugo's jaw dropped as he realized something else.

"I was wrong," he muttered. "The scar on Saddler's neck has *everything* to do with his murder! I just need to make a call."

"Wait! Wait!" I yelled.

Both Hugo and Mrs. Bradley turned to me in surprise.

"Mrs. Bradley," I demanded. "Are you licensed to carry that thing?"

I pointed to the gun still gripped in her hand, and *she* had the nerve to look at me in surprise. With the phone receiver in his hand, Hugo stared at the gun and then at Mrs. Bradley, and then back at me. I, in turn, stared at Hugo for answers.

"Oh," he started. "Oh dear… I can see how that might have been startling…with all the excitement and running out here like she did. Yes, of course…well, she *is* licensed, but I suppose you would probably think that odd—Mrs. B with a gun and all. But, well…" He agonized over what to say. "I hope you aren't uncomfortable. She really is a perfect shot."

I shook my head and fell backward onto the couch.

Mrs. Bradley shuffled over to me and patted my arm. "Handled a gun for *years*," she said, trying to comfort me. "You have to be ready for anything, living with this lug nut!" Laughing a sweet yet now incongruous grandma-like laugh, she returned calmly to her room.

Having managed to leave me in complete shock once again, Hugo refocused his attention on his phone call to Detective Shaw.

"Detective Shaw," he said into the receiver. "I've got an idea. Can you check a couple of things for me? Birth certificates and body marks…"

❧

Evening had come, and Detective Shaw had been able to provide Hugo with the information he needed to confirm his theory. The wheels had been set in motion, and an arrest had been made. Finally, I sat across from Hugo in great anticipation and with a cup of coffee nestled in my hand. I was at last going to become privy to how it had all been done and how exactly it was possible for Gordon Saddler to have died *twice*.

"You see," explained Hugo, "it was really quite simple. Here is what we know. Gordon Saddler, who died in my apartment, was released from prison years ago, but he was estranged from his family and friends. I strongly suspect this was because he was on the run from Leo Grimes. Gordon Saddler claimed the inheritance left to him by his uncle and moved into the small community of Dover Hills. From then on, he lived a modest, quiet life."

"Yes, but I still don't see how he could die Thursday and then Friday—"

Hugo lifted his palm and continued.

"It was when he appeared in the paper that everything unraveled for Mr. Saddler. Leo Grimes, seeing his name and picture, determined that Gordon Saddler was hiding out in Dover Hills and killed him. Simple, really."

Hugo stood up from his seat and paced the living room.

"This is where it gets interesting. The phone call I made to Detective Shaw was to determine if there were any distinguishing marks on the body of the Gordon Saddler who died in Dover Hills, but she confirmed that he *didn't* have any."

"How could that be?" I asked. "I remember that scar on his neck distinctly. You couldn't miss it."

"Right! Now, knowing this new information, let's start again and consider what must have actually happened. On Thursday, the killer found Mr. Saddler in Dover Hills and shot him, but after killing him, he realized that the distinctive scar wasn't there."

"Wait…so that means," I conjectured, "that it wasn't the same man, after all. You can't just make a scar disappear."

"Exactly. That's also what the killer realized."

"But the name and picture…"

Hugo smiled. "It was only when Mrs. Bradley mentioned her own sister that it occurred to me that Gordon Saddler could have a brother…a *twin* brother. Do you remember when the gardener, Mr. Finkler, told us that Old Jones had called Gordon Saddler 'a chip off the old block'?"

"I do."

"Mr. Finkler also described Old Jones as a crook. Therefore, Mr. Finkler expected Gordon Saddler to be an equally unpleasant person. He even remarked on his surprise when he met Gordon Saddler and discovered that he was a nice, honest guy. The Gordon Saddler Mr. Finkler got to know wasn't like Old Jones at all."

"So, you're saying that the Gordon Saddler of Dover Hills was actually the amicable twin brother?"

"Exactly. The *real* Gordon Saddler who died in my apartment, however, does have a criminal history and was probably very much like Old Jones. For the sake of simplicity, let us say that the Dover Hills brother was the 'good' twin, but not entirely without the Saddler gene, because when he learned of his brother's inheritance from his uncle, he decided to claim it as his own. After all, it's a small town, and he hasn't heard from his brother, Gordon, in years. He tells the town that *his* name is Gordon Saddler and lives quietly there for over a year.

"What he doesn't know, however, is that the real Gordon Saddler, who was estranged from his family, was in hiding from Leo Grimes. Unfortunately, it is because of the 'good' twin's benevolence that his picture and his brother's name appear in the paper. He has no idea that anyone is after his brother. Leo Grimes kills the 'good' twin but then realizes that there isn't a scar on his neck. Recognizing his mistake, Grimes continues to search for the correct brother. The real Gordon Saddler also sees the same newspaper article and comes to me for help."

"Why not go to the police for protection?" I asked.

Hugo shrugged. "I suspect he hadn't entirely given up his life of crime, and perhaps he had doubts that the police would be the best place to go for help. He came to me because I am a private investigator. He didn't know for sure if I would help, but I was his best chance. He burst into my apartment, but by that point, Grimes had already administered the cyanide. Gordon Saddler was a hefty man who I imagine could eat a large meal, so the poison would have taken a little longer to react."

"But *when* did Grimes poison Saddler?" I asked, standing. "I can't imagine that it was much earlier than when he arrived at your apartment."

"And I agree," said Hugo, nodding. "I suspect that Saddler came to see me immediately upon arriving in town, but I wasn't home—and nor was Mrs. Bradley—to let him in. Probably hungry, he decided to grab a bite to eat at a nearby restaurant while he waited for me to return. The closest restaurant is a little sandwich shop just down the street from here."

"I know it," I replied. "I ate there myself just before running into you."

A smile tugged at Hugo's lips. "Mr. Saddler must have been there at the same time as you—really, to be technical, he was murdered there. Leo Grime's men followed Saddler to the sandwich shop and administered the cyanide in his food."

I sank once more into my seat, astonished. Looking toward Hugo, I mumbled, "I…I had no idea. I was so engrossed in having just lost my job, I barely even made notice of the man who made my sandwich, let alone Saddler!"

Hugo shrugged. "I wouldn't have expected you to. There was nothing to alert you to the fact that a murder was going to take place."

Removing his glasses, Hugo vigorously rubbed his square lenses with a handkerchief. Blinking, he looked in my general direction and added, "You left the sandwich shop, ran into me, and together we entered my apartment. Gordon Saddler saw that I had returned home and burst in soon after. He had just enough time before he died to declare to us that 'he' had been killed the day before."

Astounded, I sat in silence for a bit before finally asking, "Do you work on these types of cases all the time?"

Hugo, looking as perplexed as always by my simplest of questions, replied, "Well, yes. I suppose I do."

Taking a sip of my coffee, I nodded thoughtfully.

At last, Hugo broke the silence. "Want to join me?"

Peering over the rim of my mug, the corner of my lip tugged upward.

"Definitely," I replied. "Definitely."

FIVE

THE STRANGE DISAPPEARANCE OF MR. WELLS

MONTHS AGO, AN unexpected reunion with my friend and private investigator Hugo Flynn had resulted in us joining our efforts to solve a rather curious case concerning one man and *both* of his deaths. That man was overambitious, if you ask me, but there it was—the case that started our partnership.

Being down on my luck at the time and having nowhere else to go, I took residence in one of Hugo's extra rooms. In exchange, I assisted my friend in his various cases, documenting some of the more interesting crimes for my periodical, the *Sleuth's Observer*. The case that I am going to expound upon now has already garnered much attention in the newspapers, but it is the lesser-known case that actually started it all that has been of particular interest to my colleague and me. I refer, of course, to the Lunford Museum Robbery.

It was the third Tuesday of July, just after breakfast, when Hugo sighed and tossed a newspaper in my direction.

"We might as well pick a crime from the headlines," he said. "We haven't had a case in *weeks*."

As I considered our options, Hugo stretched his skinny frame across the couch, the lapels of his new blazer crumpling against his chest as he pressed a pillow onto his face in anguish.

"Come now," cooed Mrs. Bradley, Hugo's irreplaceable live-in housekeeper. "It can't be as bad as all that, Huey, dear," she consoled, her wrinkled hand pouring us cups of tea. "I'm sure there will be a nice robbery—oh, or better yet, a mean old serial killer on the loose." She squeezed his shoulder encouragingly.

"Yes, Mrs. B, one can only hope," I said dryly.

Turning the paper over, I asked my friend, "How about the man who was shot to death in South Havenfield?"

Based on Hugo's muffled response, I deduced that he had little interest in that particular case.

"A robbery, perhaps?" I asked, turning the page. "Apparently, an old relic—some sort of jewelry box, dated to almost a thousand years ago—was stolen from the Lunford Archaeological Museum last night, and the archaeologists are in hysterics. They recently acquired the jewelry box, and it's worth quite a lot of money, it seems. Someone swapped the genuine artifact with a fake one when it was in transit to the museum."

I was pleased to find that this article seemed to elicit at least some interest from the detective as his face emerged from beneath the pillow.

"Any leads?" he asked.

"Authorities are looking into the two drivers that were commissioned to transport the artifact. One has apparently deposited large sums of money into his account within the last few months."

Hugo groaned and proceeded to slip back under his pillow. As terrible as it sounds, I was actually disappointed that the authorities had a viable lead, for Hugo's sake. He needed a case that would challenge him.

At the sound of the doorbell, Hugo completely dismissed my efforts and leapt up from the sofa. His dress shoes slid across the hardwood floor as he rushed to open the door.

"Oh, *please* let it be a poisoning, or maybe a political scandal…or a shocking case of double homicide!"

I sighed, knowing that Hugo's thoughts were not limited to the company of friends.

From across the threshold, I observed a rather homely looking, middle-aged woman. Her features were not remarkable by any means, with the exception of her eyes. They were sharp and alert—clever—and I recall thinking very strongly that masked behind that mundane veneer was, I expected, an incredibly intelligent woman.

I'm afraid, by way of first impression, Hugo's excitement for a scandalous affair faltered. Still, we were hopeful.

"Please, have a seat, Ms.…?"

"Mrs. Wells," she stated promptly, studying Hugo. "Julia Wells."

Gently placing the now-disheveled sofa pillow behind her, she divided her attention between the two of us.

"Oh, and this is David Merrick," introduced Hugo hastily. "A colleague of mine."

My eyes settled briefly upon Hugo as I waited for him to wave his hand in dismissal. Such a gesture, I felt, would have been fitting for such an unflattering introduction. My slight annoyance, however, was quickly extinguished as I attributed his behavior to sheer eagerness. I was proved correct when Hugo rushed over to a seat across from Mrs. Wells and immediately seized upon his quarry.

"Now, what seems to be the problem, Mrs. Wells?" he asked.

Hesitating, the client's eyelashes fluttered downward, and she watched her fingers as she plucked at a loose thread on her pant leg. Hugo, ever awkward in relating to others, "encouraged" her to speak.

"Death? Poisoning, perhaps?" he asked, hopeful. "Found a body, have we? Not sure what to do with it?"

The now-wide eyes of Mrs. Wells returned to the detective's. I fully expected Hugo's eyebrows to dart up and down in joyous anticipation.

"Please," I interjected, "share with us why you've come. As you can see"—I glanced toward Hugo reproachfully (his expression, in turn, was one of incomprehension)—"we deal with all sorts of problems. I'm sure what you've got to tell us won't be all that unfamiliar."

Studying me briefly, Mrs. Wells nodded. "All right," she began. "I suspect my husband of having an affair—"

Hugo's eager expression deflated considerably—so much so, in fact, that Mrs. Wells became mildly panicked and burst into speech.

"No, you don't understand," she reassured him. "As I said, I suspect, or perhaps *suspected* my husband of having an affair." She accepted the water offered to her by Mrs. Bradley. "The last few weeks, he has been acting so strangely. Then last night he told me he had to go somewhere for work. Not believing him, I followed him when he left the house. He pulled into a hotel."

Mrs. Wells's voice broke. Pausing, she took a sip of her water.

"Before you continue," I began, "in what way was your husband acting strangely?"

"Oh, I suppose 'strange' in the usual sense that one would expect if one's spouse were hiding something—coming home later and talking to me less...taking calls in such a way that I didn't overhear him."

I nodded. "Please continue. What happened when you followed your husband?"

"As I said, I suspected my husband of having an affair, so I discreetly followed him to the hotel room and watched as he entered. I crept closer and listened just outside the door. I heard his voice—it has a very distinct, nasal sound. Anyway, I knew he must have been talking to someone—his mistress, no doubt."

Mrs. Wells's hand shook as she took another sip of her water.

"I remember that he said, 'I've got it now. Let's go.' I waited until I could make sure there was another voice in the room. I couldn't make it out, but I was sure there was someone in there with him. I saw the housekeeper walking down the hall—she must have just finished cleaning the room next door—and I threw a fit, telling her I had locked my baby in the room and I needed her to open the door immediately because I had left the water running in the tub. That was the first thing that came to my mind to get her to open the door without any questions."

Clever, I thought.

"The maid didn't hesitate," explained Mrs. Wells. "We flung open the door, and I rushed in expecting to have my proof, and..."

She stared blankly past us, her forehead wrinkling in bewilderment.

"What happened, Mrs. Wells? What did you see?"

"Nothing," she stated.

"Come now, Mrs. Wells," I encouraged. "You can tell us. You've said this much already."

Turning her blank gaze toward mine, she repeated, "Nothing…"

Blinking past the confusion, she rubbed her head as if in pain.

"Nothing *is* what I mean to tell you. There was nothing! No one was there! Not my husband, not a mistress, not even a pulled-out chair or a glass of water to tell me that someone had at least *been* there. My husband, you see, went into that hotel room and never came out." Pinching the bridge of her nose, she added under her breath, "And I haven't seen him since."

"And this was just last night, you say?" asked Hugo.

Mrs. Wells nodded tiredly.

"Have you gone to the police?" I asked.

"I have," she replied. "But since he hasn't been gone even a full day, it's not quite at the top of their list." Turning pleadingly toward Hugo, she added, "But I was there, Mr. Flynn. I literally followed him into that room, and he never came out."

"Was there a balcony, windows?" asked Hugo.

"Yes, there were windows but no balcony. It was a room on the first floor. The windows were blocked because of some construction next door—heavy machinery obstructed the entire first floor. You can only push the window open about a foot, if that much. There is no way he could have exited through the window. The gap is too small. And before you ask, no, there was not a connecting door to any other room."

"So you are suggesting your husband just vanished?"

"Well…yes. That's *exactly* what I'm suggesting!"

❧

Hugo and I arrived at the Sleeping Willows Hotel just after ten in the morning. Set in the historic district of Havenfield, the quaint hotel was no more than three stories and still maintained much of its original architectural integrity. The owner and manager of the hotel, Mr. Charles Smedley, was, in my opinion, an odd sort of man, in both appearance and manner. He reminded me very much of one of those hairless, wrinkled cats with a wisp of thinning hair on the top of its head. His shoulders had the habit of sinking forward when he walked, and he constantly held the palms of his hands close to his chest, anxiously moving them in circles around each other. He was, however, particularly helpful, assuring us that we would have unlimited access to the room in question and expressing great sympathy for Mrs. Wells, who was accompanying us during our inquiries at the hotel.

"As you can see," explained Mr. Smedley, sliding his guest book across the table toward us, "we've got it recorded that Mr. Henry Wells reserved this room exactly one week ago." Pushing his glasses farther up the bridge of his nose, he added, "We reserved Room 102 for Mr. Wells, and he even paid for the entire week in advance. Everything checked out from our end, you see? By the book—that's how I run my hotel."

"Did he specifically ask for Room 102?" asked Hugo.

The manager shook his head. "No, he just wanted a room on the first floor—he said something about the stairs being a hassle." Shrugging, he stood. "Would you like to see the room now?"

We expressed that we would, and it was just as Mrs. Wells had described it.

"There's certainly only one way in or out," said Hugo, pressing the window open as far as possible. "It stops just short of a foot," he added, roughly measuring the gap with his forearm.

Peering out the small space through the side of his eye, he asked, "Just one other room to the left here until you reach the hotel's entryway, Mr. Smedley?"

"Yes, yes," stuttered the owner excitedly. "Facing the window, you can see the window of Room 101 to your left and, if the construction materials weren't in the way, you would be able to see the window to Room 103 to your right." Turning the keys over in his hands, he added, "We have two entrances to the hotel. One from Haven Street, where you entered from, and the other from this side." He pointed toward Hugo. "That's Lunford Avenue. Not many people have come and gone from that side, however, because of all the construction. Blocks this entire side of the first floor." Mr. Smedley's brow creased. "Not good for business. Not good for business at all."

"Who is staying in the room on the left?" asked Hugo.

Mr. Smedley reflected, his eyes blinking rapidly as he called the name to memory. "Room 101… Yes! That's Mr. Jerry Pruit. He's an older man visiting from Nebraska…or was it Nevada?" He frowned. Looking toward the detective, he added, "He's been here a little over a week now. Well, *was* here—the room is no longer occupied, if you would like to inspect it as well… although I'm not sure why that would help."

Mr. Smedley frowned once more, his mind seeming to work tirelessly on the problem.

"It's available?" I asked, bringing Mr. Smedley back to the present. "Has Mr. Pruit gone?"

The hotel owner nodded. "Checked out this morning, as a matter of fact."

Static buzzed through Mr. Smedley's radio as one of the maids called for his assistance.

"If you'll excuse me. Please let me know if there is anything you need. I will unlock Mr. Pruit's room on my way out…if you need to go in there." Turning toward Mrs. Wells, he added, "Again, Mrs. Wells, I am so very sorry for whatever has taken place." Rubbing his palm against his pant leg, he added, "It's an unusual situation, and I'm sorry it has happened at my hotel."

The manager turned away and lumbered hurriedly toward the door.

"Mrs. Wells?" asked Hugo. "You said a maid granted you access to this room. Would you locate her so that we might have a word?"

"Of course."

I watched as Mrs. Wells left the room before remarking to Hugo, "Why the interest in the adjacent room? Do you think Mr. Wells might have gone in there instead of this one? Perhaps Mrs. Wells was mistaken?"

"Possibly," replied Hugo. "But I'm more interested in its smell."

"Excuse me? The smell?" I asked, but Hugo didn't reply. He was leaning on the desk that was situated just under the window, focusing on studying the space. In deep thought, he pulled his curly hair away from his rather large forehead.

"Strong scent of citrus," he said, then quite suddenly he pushed himself off the desk and strode toward Room 101. "I don't think there is much left to see here," he remarked. "Let's take a whiff of the other room, shall we?"

"A whiff?" I asked, but Hugo was already entering the other room.

I lingered behind Hugo. This room seemed identical to the last. I discreetly took a few sniffs through my nose and thought that this room also smelled fairly clean…perhaps not *as* citrusy, but clean nevertheless. I still had no idea what significance the smell of each room could have on the case, but I knew enough not to question Hugo's tactics. They always seemed to work.

Leaning against the doorframe, I watched as Hugo pressed the window in the same manner as before, producing the same results: a one-foot gap through which a body could not squeeze in or out. Then I watched in bewilderment as he walked through the room, his nose twitching wildly like that of an excitable guinea pig.

"Interesting, very interesting," he remarked, inhaling and exhaling deeply this time. "I think that— Oh!"

Turning, I followed Hugo's startled gaze toward a considerably robust woman standing in the doorway. She had a mass of frizzy red hair restrained only by a maid's cap that was bound tightly atop her head. It was an accomplishment, I suspected, achieved only through sheer determination. I realized, of course, that she must be the maid that had assisted Mrs. Wells. The maid's flushed face was one of sincere enthusiasm, and I staggered backward as her eyes met mine, and she suddenly charged at us as if we were spectators on safari who had just gotten between a mother elephant and its baby.

"Edna Blevins," she declared, swinging her arm toward us.

With one firm shake, she took *us* aside to explain what it was we were to look for.

"A man," she stated.

"A man?" I asked.

"Why, yes! A man, and he sounded like he had a cold," she added. "I heard him say, 'Come on, hurry.'" Leaning in, Mrs. Blevins whispered, "That poor missus behind me. To have a cheatin' man. My Ben would never cheat on me, and if he ever did—woe the day!"

She thrust her arms upward, allowing her body to fall

backward into a chair. Fanning herself, she added, "That would be the day, I tell you." She narrowed one eye at us knowingly.

Hugo, startled by such a self-assured and…lively woman, remained momentarily speechless. I took the liberty of beginning my own line of inquiry.

"Mrs. Blevins—"

"Call me Ms. Edna, hun. No need to be so formal."

"Right." I cleared my throat. "Ms. Edna, can you tell us exactly what happened last night? Perhaps start a little before you made the acquaintance of Mrs. Wells, please. For instance, where were you?"

Mrs. Blevins reflected briefly, tapping a fiery-red fingernail against her cheek. "I had just finished cleaning the room next door—that's Room 103. No sooner had I pushed my cart out into the hallway than Mrs. Wells came running frantically toward me, yelling about her baby being locked in the room and the bathwater running. Needless to say, I'm a mom myself, and no babies were going up to the good Lord before their time—not on my watch! So I ran to the room and was inserting my key when I heard a man speak."

"The one who sounded like he had a cold," I said.

"Right," continued Mrs. Blevins. "I didn't have time to think it strange that a man was in there when Mrs. Wells was asking for help to get in. All I thought of was the baby. I burst through the door and made my way straight to the tub. No child! No running water!

"Needless to say, I confronted Mrs. Wells about it, and when she told me"—Mrs. Blevins lowered her voice once more—"about that cheatin' husband of hers…" She smiled encouragingly toward Mrs. Wells and continued. "Well, I just said to her, 'I don't blame you one bit.' Not one bit! She had personal business to handle, and amen to that!"

Hugo, having recovered from his initial shock, asked, "Were you responsible for cleaning Mr. Wells's room during the duration of his stay?"

Mrs. Blevins shook her head. "Normally, I would have been, because I am in charge of this entire floor. I clean each room like clockwork. The only time I won't clean a room is if the guests request as much by putting a 'Do Not Disturb' sign on the handle, or if they ask me personally when they see me in the hall."

"So, Mr. Wells had the 'Do Not Disturb' sign up all week?"

"Sure did, except for yesterday. He left a note. It asked that I air out his room because it didn't have a fresh scent. I'll tell you what I did with that note! I snatched it up from that door handle, that's what I did! Of *course* it wouldn't have a fresh scent! What does he expect if he doesn't let me clean the room?"

Mrs. Blevins stood, swung her wide hips toward Mrs. Wells, and grasped the woman's hand in hers. "I'm sorry, Mrs. Wells," she said, shaking her head sadly. "I've been trying to hold my tongue, but that husband of yours isn't worth it. No common sense, that man…and a cheatin' man at that." Mrs. Blevins shook her head solemnly once more and patted the petite hand she held in her palm. "Let him go, miss. You've just got to let him go."

Hugo coughed. "Yes, well," he began again. "Did any of the other hotel guests request that you were not to clean their room?"

"Yes, Mrs. Whitaker in Room 112," replied Mrs. Blevins, releasing her grasp on Mrs. Wells. "And Mr. Pruit from this room"—she pointed her finger toward the floor—"number

101. Mrs. Whitaker put up a sign just one day this week, and Mr. Pruit asked me personally yesterday morning when I happened to run into him in the hallway. He said he had a research project spread out all over his room and didn't want his papers disturbed. Sweet old man, Mr. Pruit. Some sort of scientist, that one, or maybe an archaeologist?" Edna nodded. "That was it, archaeologist. I remember thinking 'old bones,' digging up old bones." She grunted. "Not very nice when I say it out loud, is it? But there it is, if you want honesty. Still, I did say he is a sweet old man, didn't I?"

"Yes, you did," I replied, regaining Mrs. Blevins's attention. "Did you notice anything out of the ordinary when you were in Mr. Wells's room, or in the hallway during the time you were assisting Mrs. Wells?"

"Not a thing. When I was helping Mrs. Wells, I didn't see anyone in the hall because I was in the room with her the whole time. As for when I was cleaning his room, there wasn't anything strange there either. I opened the window like he asked, did a quick clean—"

"Using lemon-scented products?" asked Hugo.

"That's right," said Mrs. Blevins. "Then I left." She tilted her head to one side. "Although," she added slowly, "I thought one thing was odd…his bed. I didn't have to make it. I thought to myself, this man has been here an entire week, *denying* my services, and he never slept in his bed? Then I thought perhaps he had made it himself, but I doubt that. That bed was made expertly, like how I would have made it." She sniffed. "Like I said, he didn't strike me as very bright."

Mrs. Blevins glanced apologetically toward Mrs. Wells.

"And besides," she added, "makes me wonder what he had this room for if not for sleeping or reading the good Word.

Didn't want anyone to see him, whatever it was. Sinnin', no doubt. Drugs would be my guess. My mother always said—"

"Yes, well," I interjected. "Thank you very much, Mrs. Blev—excuse me, Ms. Edna. You have been more than helpful. Any other questions, Hugo?" I asked over my shoulder.

Hugo expressed that he had none. Mrs. Blevins marched out of the room, passing Mr. Smedley on her way out.

"Any headway?" asked the hotel owner as he peered over the rim of his glasses that were settled comfortably on the tip of his nose.

"Not much," I replied, feeling even more disappointed with our lack of progress as I caught a glimpse of Mrs. Wells's fallen expression.

"May I use your telephone, Mr. Smedley?" asked Mrs. Wells.

"Of course, Julia," he replied. "My office is to the left once you enter the lobby."

With a nod, Mrs. Wells excused herself, but I couldn't help but feel that my discouraging remark had provoked her sudden retreat.

"We've really got to make some sort of progress, Hugo. I feel terrible. This woman's husband is gone, and we've got nothing to tell her. I suppose we need to track down Mr. Pruit. He is the next closest witness to the case…"

Hugo smiled. "On the contrary, David, I already know exactly where Mr. Wells is."

Turning toward Mr. Smedley, Hugo remarked, "David, meet our 'Mr. Wells.' Mr. Smedley, you and your wife are soon to be under arrest."

❧

Having successfully detained both Mrs. Julia Smedley (formerly known as Mrs. Julia Wells) and Mr. Charles Smedley in the original hotel room that had claimed so much of our attention, we awaited the police's arrival. Although I was annoyed that Mrs. Smedley had drawn us into this odd farce concerning her husband's disappearance, I couldn't help but ask Hugo what exactly they had done to warrant arrest. Hugo explained.

"The search for 'Mr. Wells' actually had nothing to do with his disappearance," replied Hugo. "This whole farce of a case was simply a smoke screen to mask the real crime, which was the theft of the valuable artifact recently discovered by archaeologists. Mr. Smedley himself, not expecting us to make the connection, remarked on all the construction happening just outside on *Lunford* Avenue. Recall, David, the headline you read earlier mentioning the jewelry box that was stolen from the Lunford Museum. It is only logical that the Lunford Museum should be located on Lunford Avenue. Now, let me explain how it was done."

Mr. Charles Smedley shifted uncomfortably in his seat.

"Edna, the maid, takes great pride in her work, and as such, she cleans each room (unless otherwise asked) with a systematic diligence. In her own words, she operates like 'clockwork.' As a result, Mr. Smedley and his wife knew exactly when to expect Edna to finish cleaning Room 103, as well as when she would proceed down the hall to clean the room of 'Mr. Wells,' Room 102. Remember, it was only that morning that 'Mr. Wells' had requested the window be left open to air. Edna made her way down the hall and ran into the supposed Mrs. Wells, who is really Mrs. Julia Smedley. 'Mrs. Wells' convinced Edna to unlock the room with her phony story of a child in danger, but only after she was certain that Edna had heard the distinct voice of her husband, Mr. Wells, coming from inside the room. The pair burst through the door, and Edna hurried into the bathroom to rescue the infant she expected to find in the bathtub, and there is no doubt in my mind that Edna, being such a spirited woman, rushed toward the bathroom without even glancing at the rest of the room."

I nodded strongly in agreement as Hugo continued.

"'Mrs. Wells,' however, did not go toward the bathroom. She headed straight to the open window, which is just above the writing desk. Mr. Wells—who is really Mr. Charles Smedley dressed in disguise—was standing outside the window on Lunford Avenue at the same time that his wife was employing their charade with the maid. Recall, the window only opens far enough to fit something through that is a foot wide or less. So, at the appropriate time, Mr. Smedley had slipped what I believe to be the most logical tool—a recorder—through the window and onto the desk, thus creating the voice Edna heard just before storming in. Mrs. Wells collected the recorder and hid it in her purse before meeting Edna in the bathroom to explain the real reason she had made her enter the room—to catch her cheating husband. Edna, ever sympathetic to the cause, spent time counseling Mrs. Wells, no doubt, and inadvertently remained in the room and out of sight of what was going on in the hallway."

"So, I'm assuming," I conjectured, "that while Mrs. Wells was distracting Edna, Mr. Wells was on Lunford Avenue obtaining the fake jewelry box from the same driver who was recently paid large sums of money. Just as the newspapers reported."

"Exactly," replied Hugo. "Making sure, of course, to use the distinct voice of Mr. Wells while he spoke with the driver. This ensured that when the driver, once caught, talked to the police, he would describe the man the Smedleys *wanted* him to describe—a man by the name of Mr. Wells, with a nasal voice. The same man who occupied Room 102 but has since vanished. Edna would also confirm that she, too, heard the same man. An independent investigation was even done by his wife to try and find him!"

"But then why," I asked, "did they have to keep Edna out of the hallway? After receiving the jewelry box from the driver, all Mr. Smedley would have to do is get away, right?"

Hugo shook his head. "Not if they were going to use 'Mr. Wells' as their fall guy. Most likely, there would be witnesses or perhaps even security cameras outside the hotel. The couple counted on that. Mr. Smedley, in disguise as Mr. Wells, made the switch with the security guard and was seen on camera walking back into the hotel. So now the police would narrow their search down to someone staying at the hotel.

"Here is where this ruse of the vanishing husband became essential. 'Mr. Wells,' with the stolen jewelry box, came into the hotel and proceeded down the first-floor hallway. He was no longer under surveillance. As the actual owner of the hotel, he made sure of that.

"Instead of entering Room 102, where Edna and Mrs. Wells were located, he entered *Mr. Pruit's* room in 101, still dressed as Mr. Wells. He couldn't have anyone see him enter that room dressed as Mr. Wells, especially the opinionated Edna. So 'Mrs. Wells' continued to keep Edna occupied. This was essential because now that the jewelry box had been stolen, they needed the suspicion to fall on Mr. Wells who disappeared from Room *102.*"

"Mr. Pruit never really existed either!" I exclaimed.

Hugo smiled. "No. It's rather easy to play an old man, isn't it, Mr. Smedley? A white beard that covers the face, a cane, and perhaps a slow, careful walk around the hotel to convince the other guests and employees that old Mr. Pruit is staying in Room 101? The following morning, you checked out as the kindly old man who had nothing to do with the robbery, which would have been discovered that very morning. Everything would point back to the mysterious Mr. Wells.

"Furthermore, Mr. Smedley, you made sure you personally requested that Edna was not to clean your room on the day of the robbery so she would have no chance of discovering your disguise or the stolen jewelry box. That's also why Mr. Pruit's room didn't smell as strongly of cleaning products."

"That's why you were sniffing both rooms," I remarked.

"Exactly," replied Hugo. "I thought it was curious that one room would smell so strongly of cleaning products but the room next to it wouldn't. That meant at least one occupant requested that the maid not enter his room. Under normal circumstances, that would simply be explained by a guest's preference for privacy. However, considering the museum robbery and Mr. Wells's strange disappearance, I had to consider every detail—even the maid's comings and goings. Of course, later we confirmed from Edna that during the entire week of Mr. Wells's stay, he only made one request for her to clean his room—the day of the robbery—and he specifically asked that she air the room out by *opening the window*, which was ultimately crucial for their plan to work."

I must admit, I was completely dumbfounded by the connection Hugo made between the two crimes. To Hugo, however, it was only logical. Having sorted all the information and, most importantly, having not discounted the seemingly unimportant information about the robbery he had heard of earlier, he was able to find the true motive.

Hugo looked curiously at the odd, catlike husband who sat anxiously in the corner.

"It was really all the wife's idea, of course. Mr. Smedley strikes me as a man of weak resolve, and when he mentioned that the museum construction had been bad for business, I imagined the temptation to steal a valuable artifact that was just across the street was far too great for him to ignore. However, it was his wife's cunning that made the plan possible."

"But how could you have possibly known we were married?" asked Mrs. Smedley.

"It was the familiarity with which your husband said your name, Mrs. Smedley," explained Hugo. "That's what gave me the final connection I needed. Do you recall when you asked to use the phone? Mr. Smedley called you by your first name, with a familiarity that was far too natural. I thought, *What if these two actually know each other?* And once I started on that line of thought, the pieces fell swiftly into place!"

Mr. Smedley apologized to his wife, and she consoled him with a reassuring strength.

"We endeavored to do what we needed to, dear," she whispered, "and you and I won't apologize for that."

In a way, I found her constitution admirable (if only it weren't so misguided). Turning toward Mrs. Smedley, I asked, "Why in the world did you come to us for help? If you hadn't, you probably would have gotten away with it!"

"For credibility," she replied. "I needed to show the police that I, Mrs. Wells, had done all I could to find my husband, to make them believe that Mr. Wells was real...a man with a family and people who knew him. Once they turned their attention to searching for Mr. Wells, I would have removed this mundane attire. Mrs. Wells would have disappeared, and I would have returned to being myself. The police would be searching for someone who doesn't exist. We would have been in the clear."

Still dressed as Mrs. Wells, Mrs. Smedley rose and removed the brown wig and shrugged herself free from the faded overcoat that engulfed her. It was now that I saw the full embodiment of the woman who lived behind the intelligent eyes upon which I had earlier remarked. Turning toward Hugo, she added, "I had no idea, Mr. Flynn, that you would be this good."

Hugo, true to form, stammered an incoherent, embarrassed thank you. His brows pinched together in bewilderment. Compliments, be they indirect or otherwise, always managed to baffle the sleuth.

"I think the police have arrived," I remarked, standing. Turning to Hugo, I smiled, adding, "If you will excuse me, the *Sleuth's Observer* has breaking news to report."

SIX
A DEADLY REFERRAL

TIRES SCREECHED ACROSS the pavement just outside Private Investigator Hugo Flynn and my apartment building, jolting me awake. I scrambled from my bed, shivering as my bare feet struck the cold, hardwood floor.

"The driver must be right outside!" yelled Hugo as he rushed into the hallway, nearly colliding into me.

The sound of crunching metal and shattering glass thundered in my ears. My fingers trembled as I struggled to pull on my shoes, then I followed Hugo onto the concrete stoop of our building. I staggered back, hit by the stench of burning rubber. Coughing, I pulled the collar of my shirt over my nose and peered through the darkness of the early-morning hour. Smoke hissed as it streamed from the car's engine, stinging my eyes, but I could make out Hugo's tall figure under the flickering yellow hue of the streetlamp. I called the police, then joined him at the driver's side door.

"Can you hear me, sir?" asked Hugo as he checked the driver's pulse through the car's broken window.

The man's eyes fluttered only briefly in response. His dark hair was damp and matted just above his temple. Hugo forced the man's seat buckle loose, its strap having tightened uncomfortably against his chest. The driver drew in several short, labored breaths.

"What is your name, sir?" asked Hugo.

The man's narrowed eyes searched Hugo's face as he struggled to reply. Hugo encouraged the man to speak, to stay with him as he checked his body for obvious abrasions.

"F... F... F..." The man's swollen lip stifled his reply.

"That's right, sir. Just stay with me!" repeated Hugo.

Hugo looked at me from over his shoulder. "Give me your shirt, David," he instructed. "I need some pressure here." He held his hands tightly around the upper part of the driver's left arm. I fumbled with the fabric, my fingers tense as I forced an untidy knot around the wound.

"F... Fl..." The driver struggled to speak once more.

"I hear the sirens," said Hugo as he yanked at the mangled car door, but it only moved as far as the crushed hinges would allow—mere inches at a time.

"All right, now try," I said as I dug in my heels and pulled as well, glass crunching under my shoes. Hugo leaned his slender frame against the inside of the door, and we moved it away from the driver's limp body as much as we could.

"*Flynn...*" The driver's voice was like crushed gravel.

Hugo crouched beside him. "*Who are you?*" asked Hugo, staring at the man's bruised lips as though willing them to answer. "Who *are* you?"

I watched the driver's heaving chest slow.

"Inside…" whispered the driver, pulling a gold ring from his left hand. "Remember, Flynn? Zero…nine…one…seven… two…zero…one…eight… *Remember*…"

Hugo pressed his bloodstained fingers against the driver's as he took the ring. Flashing lights cast shadows across the driver's face as paramedics pulled their equipment through the debris, but I knew…*we* knew that it was too late.

✍

Finally, we were back inside our apartment, and I watched as Hugo scrubbed his hands forcefully under steaming hot water, the last traces of the driver's blood running into the bathroom sink.

"There was nothing we could have done, you say?" replied Hugo at my attempt to console him.

"That's right," I said as the sirens faded into the distance. "There was nothing we could have done to save him. I doubt anyone could have survived that crash…"

Leaning forward against the sink, Hugo's messy, curly hair fell over his large forehead.

"I wish he hadn't died," he murmured.

"If you're feeling some sort of guilt—" I started, uncertain of the effect this tragedy might have on Hugo or, more specifically, on his brilliant mind. Hugo Flynn was incredibly intelligent, yet he processed everyday life and personal trials differently than most. It was often difficult for one to relate to him.

I stepped toward him.

"Perhaps we should talk to someone about it… It's not an easy thing to go through."

I paused as my friend's expression hardened. Hugo lifted his eyes, peering intensely over the top of his glasses. "Nothing to do now but solve it," he said and strode past me.

"I'm unclear, Hugo," I called after him. "Solve *what*, exactly?"

Across the dimly lit living room, Hugo stooped over his antique writing desk and pulled the top drawer swiftly toward him.

"It was a car accident, Hugo," I said. "Yes, the driver *seemed* to know you, but many people do now—you've solved a lot of cases…"

Hugo made no reply. He simply pulled on the next drawer, more forcefully this time, scattering its contents onto the floor.

"*Perhaps*," I urged more loudly, now standing mere feet from my friend, "we may attempt to face traumatic events by doing what comes most naturally to us…to mask how upsetting something has been to us."

Hugo's hands grasped at yet another drawer. My head throbbed.

"Hugo!" I shouted.

Hugo's head shot upward, and as he looked at me, his eyes widened. I debated as to whether he was surprised by the fact that I had yelled, or that I was even in the room!

"Hugo," I demanded, "I am trying to ask if you are *okay*."

Confusion swept across the detective's face.

"Why wouldn't I be?" he asked, stunned.

"Because a man you tried to save died in a horrific car crash just hours ago!"

"No." Hugo shook his head. "No, he didn't."

I was taken aback, to say the least.

"Do…do you mean to say that the man is, in fact, *alive*?"

"No," replied the detective, still rummaging through the desk. "He is quite dead." Abruptly, he straightened. "Weren't you *there*?"

"Yes, Hugo!" I pinched the bridge of my nose and took a deep breath. "Of course I was there, but why are you saying he didn't *die*?"

"No, no." Hugo shook his head adamantly as he dumped out the contents of the bottom desk drawer, pawing his long fingers through the pile, his eyes still cast downward. "What I meant was that he didn't die from the *crash*."

Hugo pulled a soiled cocktail napkin from the clutter. Folding it into his pocket, he turned toward me.

"It was the bullet that killed him."

Speechless, I watched as Hugo threw a jacket over his shoulders and exited our apartment.

Lead Detective Sophia Shaw closed the meeting room door behind her and slid a file folder across the table toward us. My head was throbbing, as I had had little opportunity to sleep before Hugo called me and requested that I meet him at the police station. Of course, he had told me little to nothing, and, to be frank, I was rather annoyed about it all.

"Mr. David Merrick, it's nice to see you again."

"Detective Shaw," I replied, secretly admiring her bronzed skin and a small patch of freckles that rested on the bridge of her nose. She, I decided, was the only pleasant part of the last several hours.

"My officers were a bit surprised to see you so early this morning, Mr. Flynn," she said to Hugo. Only as the briefest of smiles swept across her face did I notice she had the faint hint of an accent.

"No time to waste," he replied, opening the file folder.

I threw back my head, swallowing a couple of aspirin as

Hugo thumbed through photographs of the accident that I had absolutely no desire to review—the scene was still fresh in my mind.

Detective Shaw took a seat across from us, her expression stoic.

"You probably know about as much as we do at this point," she remarked. "With the exception of the cause of death, I'd expect, *although...*" Detective Shaw considered Hugo for a moment. "You probably already know that the driver was shot, don't you?"

"Just below the rib cage, right side," said Hugo.

"Right, of course." Detective Shaw arched her brow in my direction. "Now, don't get me wrong," she added, turning her eyes back to Hugo. "The accident wasn't pretty, but it's the bullet that actually killed him, and I expect that's why you're here?"

Hugo nodded, closing the file. "Yes, but it's really because I should have solved the case the first time."

Detective Shaw and I exchanged glances.

"The first time?" I asked. "So you do know this man?"

"Vaguely." Hugo leaned back in his chair. "Do you recall the series of numbers he recited to us before he died?"

"I do," I replied, reaching into my jacket pocket. "I scribbled them down last night. The driver told you to remember them, so I thought I should—"

Hugo waved his hand. I paused, my hand still poised in my jacket.

"No?" I asked. "You don't want the numbers he asked you to remember?"

"I do," said Hugo. "But it wasn't just the numbers he was asking me to remember. He was also asking me *if* I remembered."

I took a slow, deep breath and turned to Detective Shaw. "Are three aspirins too many?"

Hugo pulled an envelope from his pocket. "The driver gave this to me as he was dying."

Detective Shaw's lips thinned. "That's evidence, Flynn."

"Quite."

Detective Shaw rubbed her temples. I slid my bottle of aspirin toward her.

"Just tell me what you've found out," she mumbled.

"When the driver recited those numbers," explained Hugo, "I suppose, in one way, he was asking me to remember them, but what was even more significant was that I remembered *him*."

Turning the envelope upside down, a simple gold wedding band fell out and rolled across the table.

"I met the driver a little over two years ago, around the end of March," said Hugo. "I was at the airport, waiting for my flight to leave, and I took a seat at a restaurant near to my gate. The only seats available were at the bar beside a gentleman—the driver from last night."

Hugo tapped the file folder.

"The man, for some odd reason, felt compelled to make conversation." Hugo's eyebrows wrinkled; he was genuinely perplexed by this concept. Shaking his head, he continued. "I can still tell you our conversation to this day—word for word. It intrigued me greatly. His name was Dr. Kenneth Ballard."

Hugo rested his arms across his chest. Staying true to his word, he recounted their conversation as if it had only occurred yesterday.

"Dr. Ballard asked me some questions—where I was from, where I was going…" Hugo shrugged. "Why he needed to know this information was beyond me."

I sighed. "It was small talk, Hugo."

"It was tiring is what it was," he said as he picked lint from his sleeve. "Anyway, he eventually asked me about my work. Of course, I explained I was a private detective, and he seemed particularly intrigued by this. I agreed to listen to an experience that was troubling him—if only to avoid any more meaningless conversation—and he told me about something that had occurred with one of his patients. Dr. Ballard was a primary care physician, and apparently an elderly man had come to see him at his office. The man was a walk-in by the name of Groff."

Hugo thought back a moment and nodded.

"Yes, the patient's name was Harold Groff. The doctor had a cancellation and agreed to fit the man into his schedule. During the appointment, Dr. Ballard determined that the patient's chief complaints were night sweats, anxiety, and restlessness. He hadn't slept well for weeks. So, Dr. Ballard asked the patient if there had been any recent life changes that could be contributing to his change in mood, any possible causes for his stress.

"This is where it gets interesting." Hugo leaned forward and rested his elbows on the table. "The patient pulled a crinkled sheet of paper from his pocket and read it aloud. 'To Do'—that part was underlined, and the rest that followed said, 'Go to doctor to save you. Tell him about the numbers.' The doctor asked the patient what he meant by 'save you,' but apparently the patient just stared at his 'To Do' list as though he were also trying to figure out what it meant.

"The next thing the patient did," Hugo went on, "was mutter the numbers that were written on the paper, but not in the ordinary way you'd expect. He didn't just list them—he read them very slowly, looking intensely ahead as though he were visualizing them. So, the doctor waited for him to finish and made a note of the numbers on his clipboard."

Hugo stood up from his seat and moved excitedly around the conference room.

"As Dr. Ballard told me the story, he pulled a pen from his pocket and scribbled zero, four, one, seven, two, zero, one, and six onto a cocktail napkin—*this* napkin."

Hugo pulled from his own pocket the very crumpled napkin he had searched his desk for earlier that morning and placed it beside the gold ring.

"The elderly man," continued Hugo, "apparently kept repeating those numbers again and again. In fact, the doctor couldn't get him to stop. By now, of course, I was finding his story of great interest. Unfortunately, Dr. Ballard said the patient started to escalate. He kept yelling the numbers as though something terrible was going to happen, and he asked the doctor again and again if he could save him.

"Dr. Ballard's medical assistant rushed into the exam room to help, and just as his staff started to call security, a man dressed in ordinary clothes came rushing in, claiming to know the elderly man. He was from a nursing home—Sunny Hills…or, no…" Hugo scratched his head. "I think it was Sunny Creek Nursing Home."

Detective Shaw scribbled the name in her notebook.

"Apparently," continued Hugo, "the nursing home was just a few doors down from the doctor's office. The man who claimed to know the patient explained to the doctor that Mr. Groff wasn't lucid and he had come to escort him back to the nursing home. The doctor felt uncomfortable with the whole incident, and he made sure that Mr. Groff was indeed taken safely back to the nursing home. The doctor, however, was convinced that, although the man clearly wasn't well, there was something behind what he had been saying. There was something he had wanted to express that was trapped in his muddled mind. The doctor asked me if I could make anything of it."

Hugo threw up his hands and looked back and forth between both Detective Shaw and me.

"I found his story fascinating," said Hugo, "but soon I had to leave for my flight, and he for his. I had no time to consider his case further. When I arrived home a little over a week later, I had forgotten all about the doctor and what he had told me. Unpacking, I found the cocktail napkin, but I was already buried in new cases. Still, for whatever reason—perhaps it was the mere fact that this matter remained unsolved—I saved it. Initially, I didn't recognize the driver in the accident as the same doctor I'd met two years ago, but it was when he stated the series of numbers—and, more specifically, the *way* in which he stated the numbers—that I realized he wanted me to remember him and the story he'd told me. As a matter of fact, I believe he was on his way to see me."

Detective Shaw motioned her hand toward the ring.

"And this?" she asked.

"Dr. Ballard gave me this ring as he was dying," said Hugo. "As I've shown you, it's just an ordinary gold ring, yet it must mean something significant."

"Marriage?" I asked, thinking of the first logical symbolism of a gold ring, not to mention having observed Dr. Ballard remove it from his left hand.

"Perhaps," said Hugo. "That was also my first thought. It is certainly a wedding band, and we could simply conclude that it signifies marriage…were it not for one small detail."

Hugo rotated the ring between his fingers so that we could see the inside.

"It's an engraved ring," he said. "And the difference between a plain gold marriage band and one that's engraved is that the numbers etched on the inside represent a significant date for the couple. I believe the date is the 'clue' that Dr. Ballard left for me. Perhaps it's this specific date on the ring—November 4—or *perhaps*, and this is what I believe, the clue is the *concept* of dates in general." Hugo smirked. "And here's why."

Hugo pulled a newspaper from his coat pocket.

"I obtained this from the library archives before arriving here."

Stretching the paper across the table, I read the date at top.

"'April 17, 2016,'" I read aloud, assuming that the date must be important after having just discussed the significance of the engraved ring.

"What's so important about this paper?" asked Detective Shaw, skimming the headlines.

Hugo turned to the obituaries, in which he had already circled a specific column. It read:

Mr. Harold Groff died on April 17, 2016, at the age of 83. Harold is survived by his only son, Roger Groff. He is preceded in death by his wife, Louise Groff. He leaves behind a successful shipping company and will be sorely missed by the residents and staff of the local shelter for the homeless where he volunteered much of his time. A funeral is scheduled for...

"Okay," I said. "This elderly man died..."

"Oh! I see." Detective Shaw drew the paper closer. "Mr. Harold Groff was Dr. Ballard's elderly patient, the one he spoke to you about."

"That's right," said Hugo, a grin stretching across his face. "And what's more…"

Hugo borrowed Detective Shaw's pen, his hand moving quickly as he scribbled across the soiled cocktail napkin. Lifting his head, he smiled and slid the napkin toward us. Hugo had drawn dashes between the series of numbers as followed: *04 / 17 / 2016.*

Detective Shaw gasped. My eyes darted between the dates on Mr. Groff's obituary and the tattered napkin. "It's the date the man died," I said, breathless.

"Precisely!" Hugo slapped his hand on the table. "The series of numbers Mr. Groff told Dr. Ballard indicated a date—*this* date." Hugo held up the obituary column. "Dr. Ballard, already troubled by his initial meeting with Mr. Groff, and undoubtedly curious about the significance of the numbers, must have made the same connection we did." Hugo sighed and dropped back into his chair. "Unfortunately, I think Dr. Ballard stumbled upon something he shouldn't have and tried to come to me, but the gunshot wound tells us that whoever is involved got to him first."

"So, these numbers—" said Detective Shaw, pointing to her notepad. "The numbers that Dr. Ballard recited to you last night must also be a date…"

"That's right," said Hugo.

I placed dashes between the numbers just as Hugo had done with his first set of numbers from so long ago: *09 / 17 / 2018.*

"September 17, 2018." I frowned. "But that's two weeks from now," I said, lifting my eyes.

Hugo reclined in his chair and brushed his fingers across his chin thoughtfully.

"More specifically," he said, "that's the date that someone is going to die."

⁂

"Welcome, gentlemen. Please, have a seat."

Hugo and I took seats across from the owner of Sunny Creek Nursing Home. He was a burly African American man of about sixty, and the sides of his eyes wrinkled as he smiled.

"I've heard of you, of course," remarked Mr. Dennis Williams as he reclined in his office chair, its worn leather surrendering to his stocky frame. "You're a famous sleuth—like those gumshoes my wife reads about in her novels who run around making deductions in elementary school, isn't it?" Mr. Williams frowned. "Now, that can't be right..." He scratched at the white hairs of his closely shaven beard.

"Excuse me, sir," I said. "We don't want to take too much of your time—"

Dennis Williams extended his hand across the desk.

"And you must be the trusty sidekick?" he asked, gripping my hand in his. "I've seen Mr. Flynn's photo often enough, but you...?" He paused.

"David Merrick," I replied. "Every great sleuth needs a sidekick."

"Right you are, boy! Right you are! Tell me"—he leaned forward—"what sleuth was it who had that funny little hat—had flaps that went both ways, front and back, wasn't it?" Mr. Williams's grin widened in recollection. "Where is your deerstalker cap, young man?" he exclaimed, turning toward Hugo, his round belly rumbling as his hearty laugh filled the small, cluttered office. "Better yet, where is the body?" Mr. Williams wheezed as his cheerful laughter proved too much for his round frame.

"As a matter of fact," said Hugo as Mr. Williams reached for his water. "You already know. Our business here concerns a previous resident of yours by the name of Harold Groff. He died about two years ago."

"That's what I thought," remarked Mr. Williams, clearing his throat. "Had a Detective Shaw by here not too long ago asking some questions about Mr. Groff as well." He cut a look from the side of his eye. "I figured you were here for the same reason, but I always like to let others talk first. It's not the best practice, in my opinion, to just give information away, particularly when it concerns the privacy of my residents."

His expression was serious now. Mr. Williams's chair protested as the weight of his body shifted forward, his fingers tapping anxiously within his clasped hands.

"Detective Shaw tells me you all have reason to believe that Mr. Groff died under suspicious circumstances. I'll tell you what I told her. I take the care and safety of my residents very seriously, and if you think there is anything suspicious going on here, I want to know about it. Still, I can't imagine that anything is going on in my nursing home. I take precautions against those sorts of things—the things you see on the news that make you sick to your stomach, when loved ones are abused or taken advantage of."

Mr. Williams's face twisted in disgust.

"What precautionary measures do you have in place?" I asked.

"State-of-the-art security," he replied proudly. "I've got

cameras installed in every part of this building." His chair squeaked as he swiveled left, then right, pointing in various directions. "That is, of course, with the exception of the residents' personal rooms—for privacy reasons. We document every person who comes in and out of my nursing home. Any visitors are signed in, with proper proof of identification, of course, and we only allow visitation during certain hours—again, for the safety of the residents. In case of any emergencies, I will personally escort a loved one to visit their family member, even if it's after hours."

"What about staff?" asked Hugo. "Do they have access to the facility at all times?"

"Only as necessary," replied Mr. Williams. "But even that is regulated. We have set hours for the staff, and nurses are assigned only to a select number of residents. We also have the staff log in for every shift—both coming in and going out. Once every month, we review those logs against the surveillance video." Mr. Williams lifted his chin. "Like I said, we take care of our residents. It seems doubtful that what you're saying could be true…"

"If you wouldn't mind," requested Hugo, "we would like your permission to interview some of the staff—discreetly, of course."

Mr. Williams nodded. "That's all right. I want this business sorted out as quickly as possible. I already gave Detective Shaw all I could on Mr. Groff. Just let me know if you need anything else," he said, standing.

Hugo tugged at his blazer as he, too, stood. "Mr. Williams, what can you tell me about Mr. Groff? About his personality, his likes, dislikes…"

"It's a bit fuzzy now, but I remember him being a very

nice man." Mr. Williams rested his hands on his hips, tapping a finger on the side of his belt as he recollected. "And very bright. Smart fellow. He got along well with all the staff and residents. He even helped to manage group activities. Mr. Groff was responsible for distributing flyers into the cubbies—they're sort of like mailboxes for our residents. He set up the weekly activity board, read out the bingo balls, that sort of thing. Good guy. Always involved."

Opening the door, Mr. Williams called to his receptionist.

"Ms. Helms, please give these gentlemen any information they require."

Turning, his gaze moved between Hugo and me.

"I've got a small staff," he remarked. "You might want to have a chat with Nurse Long first. She was Mr. Groff's nurse. She could tell you the most about Mr. Groff and his day-to-day activities."

❧

At the front desk, Hugo and I waited as sheets of paper hummed through the printer. Donna Helms, a woman in her fifties and Mr. Williams's receptionist, stood with her brightly painted fingernails poised over the tray. She puckered her lips and scrutinized us through distrusting eyes.

"I've got all of the staff schedules printing for the rest of this week," she remarked. Looking us up and down, she fluffed an already sizeable patch of teased blonde and gray hair that rested proudly on her head, much like a poodle's. "Anything I should be concerned about?" she asked as one of her eyebrows rose.

"Not at all," Hugo assured her. "We are simply making a few inquiries."

Ms. Helms handed us the stack of paper. "Nurse Long is here, but the rest are coming in a little later."

"Who is this—Matthew Belton?" asked Hugo, referring to his copy of the schedule. "Just comes in on evenings."

"Oh, Matt! He's the custodian. Mr. Williams arranged for him to just work later shifts—he juggles another job during the day."

"Does he have access to the residents' rooms for cleaning?" I asked.

Ms. Helms straightened the horse-themed calendar on her desk. "No, Mr. Williams calls in a professional team that sanitizes the rooms regularly. Matt just covers the general cleaning in the main areas."

"How about a Dr. Kenneth Ballard?" asked Hugo. "Did a doctor by that name ever visit here?"

The receptionist's eyes lit up.

"As a matter of fact, he did. *Handsome* man." Ms. Helms fluffed her poodle puff. "The first time he came to visit was just after sweet old Mr. Groff passed. I felt bad telling him that Mr. Groff was no longer with us. He seemed pretty upset by it, asked me a lot about him—how he liked living here, what he enjoyed doing. Mr. Groff was a good friend of his father's, apparently, and he was hoping to talk with him about old times."

I glanced toward Hugo doubtfully.

"Saw him just yesterday, as a matter of fact," Ms. Helms went on. "He's become one of our regular volunteers here."

"And did he volunteer in any part of the nursing home in particular?" asked Hugo.

Ms. Helms considered a moment. "Actually, yes…"

Rolling back in her desk chair, Ms. Helms retrieved a log-in book from her filing cabinet. Flipping through to the end, her bright-red fingernail dragged across the page.

"Here it is," she said, lifting her eyes. "He always requested to work in the activities room."

Hugo nodded thoughtfully.

"Does anyone else visit fairly regularly who's not on staff?" I asked.

"Just visitors to see the residents," answered Ms. Helms. "The only other people are family of the staff. The custodian's son, Kyle, comes by every now and again. Nice young man, although he seemed a bit anxious last time I saw him. I told him to lay off the caffeine, but he said it was finals week." Ms. Helms raised both her arms. "Who am I to argue with that boy's coffee habit? Poor thing already struggles to pay his tuition, God bless him. And don't you know those schools are *big* business! I told him he better go right ahead and pass those classes the first time 'round! I brought him a cup of coffee myself that day. If it's caffeine you need, then—"

"Anyone else?" I asked.

Ms. Helms replied immediately. "Simon Long."

Hugo glanced at me.

"He's Nurse Long's brother," she went on. "*Complete* opposites, those two. When you meet her, you'll see what I mean. She's as quiet as can be, which I don't trust." Ms. Helms crossed her arms. "Just as much as I don't trust people who talk too much without good reason. They're trying to distract you, mark my words. Now her brother"—Ms. Helms shook her head disapprovingly—"he's a bad one. Always manages to get into trouble. Been to jail twice already." She lifted two fingers for emphasis. "*Twice.*"

"Really?" I replied. "Now that is interesting."

"That's right," confirmed Ms. Helms. "But the family always

bails him out somehow. Theft, I think it was. Personally, I don't think he should be allowed in here, but he comes to visit his sister, so what can I say? Mr. Williams tends to give people the benefit of the doubt." She cast me a dubious glance. "Mr. Williams says everything is locked up that needs to be. Of course, Nurse Long's brother isn't allowed near any of the residents' rooms or anything like that, but still, I don't like it. Mr. Williams likes to remind me that we must be considerate of Nurse Long, being that he is her family." Ms. Helms arched her brow at us. "Brother, sister, cousin. Does that make him any less a thief?" Her lips puckered again as she fanned herself vigorously with a thin stack of papers from her desk.

The office phone rang, demanding the receptionist's attention. Collecting the receiver, Ms. Helms turned toward us with a final word of advice. "Love people, but don't be stupid about it, you hear?" Smiling, she greeted her caller.

Having gone in search of Nurse Long, Hugo and I caught sight of her through the open door of one of the resident's rooms.

"I'm done with these pills," complained the resident from his bed. "They get stuck on the back of your tongue and they taste awful—just awful! Take it away!"

A small plastic cup was pinched between Nurse Long's fingertips. Sighing, she rubbed at the back of her neck and caught sight of us in the doorway. Curious, she indicated that she'd be right with us.

"Mr. Riley," she tried once more. "You are under doctor's orders to take your medication. Let's try the technique I taught you so the pill doesn't touch your tongue."

Nurse Long seemed a sort of mousy individual, in both look and mannerism. She flushed as she negotiated with her patient, the tone of her fair pinkish skin deepening as the elderly man slurred insults under his breath.

"I certainly can't imagine her committing murder," I mumbled to Hugo as we waited for her in the hall.

"Why?" asked Hugo, surprised.

"Well, look at her," I argued. "She can't even stand up to that old grouch."

"David, she's *exactly* the type who could kill. Passive, meek. And what better motivation to redirect her frustration than to kill that obstinate man in his sleep? Never have to worry about him swallowing another monstrous pill again!"

"You see things in such a dismal way, Hugo!" I exclaimed.

Hugo appeared perplexed.

"Not at all!" he countered sharply. "I don't see anything less than what actually is! It is the very nature of man we're up against, David. Crime is just the symptom. Why, then, should it surprise me that a wife who has been building up hatred in her heart against her husband chooses to kill him with a blow to his head, or a nephew waits hopefully for his wealthy aunt to die? Man has free will, David, and I simply acknowledge that with free will come acts of good and, unfortunately, also acts of evil. The meek Nurse Long can make her choice just as capably as those of a more assertive disposition."

"Perhaps your perspective is a product of your profession," I said, "but I think your outlook is a bit cynical all the same."

"Perhaps," said Hugo with a shrug. "But right now, someone in this very nursing home has already caused two deaths that we know of, and it could very well be that seemingly feeble creature shoving pills down an old man's throat."

"Oh, come now!" I laughed. "I hardly think she has the capacity to shove *anything* down anyone's—"

"Sorry about the wait."

My rebuttal was interrupted as Nurse Long emerged from the room and closed the door behind her.

"Mr. Riley is always a bit…difficult," she remarked. Shifting her gaze between us, she added, "I suppose your visit concerns Mr. Groff?"

"That's right," I said, "but how did you—"

"Ms. Helms does well keeping us all abreast of the happenings here." Her cheeks reddened. "I hope that doesn't violate any police procedure."

Hugo handed her his card. "Not at all. I'm a private investigator. I merely assist the police as necessary. And this," he added, turning toward me, "is my colleague, David Merrick."

"It's a pleasure," I said. "Our meeting shouldn't take long, as we only hope to obtain a bit more information about Mr. Harold Groff."

"Of course."

Nurse Long directed us toward a round table in the staff break room. "We can talk here, although I'm not sure how much help I can be," she said, taking a seat. "It was some time ago that I cared for Mr. Groff—almost two years, I'd say."

I studied Nurse Long from across the table. With an unsteady hand, she pulled her thin hair behind her ear, her large, misty eyes staring into Hugo's.

"That's all right, Nurse Long," started Hugo. "If you could you please provide us with any information you can recall concerning Mr. Groff, that would help. Tell us about his personality, family life…"

"Of course," she said, shifting in her seat. "Mr. Groff was with us a rather long time. I'd say at least four years. From the start, he was quite friendly—a sociable man. Used to own a business and did very well for himself, if I remember correctly." She tugged absently at a loose thread on her sleeve. "He had a son, but Mr. Groff's wife had already passed away by the time he arrived here."

"Do you think he enjoyed his time at the nursing home?" asked Hugo.

"I would say so. He participated in group activities each week. Always talked to the cook to see what meal she was making for the evening. That made her feel good. I pretended I didn't notice the extra desserts he'd have on his tray." Nurse Long smiled fondly. "He was like that—the sort of man who said hi to you even if he didn't know you. Made you feel important. Really, Mr. Groff was quite an able man," she said decidedly, "but he did show signs of dementia, which is why his son brought him here. We were glad to have him with us. We just had to keep him on medication to help improve his cognitive function. Over time, it gradually got worse, though, which, unfortunately, is the case with progressive dementia. Still, he often had many lucid days."

"Do you recall an incident when Mr. Groff left this facility and went to the nearby doctor's office?" asked Hugo.

"I do, actually! Mr. Williams—he owns this nursing home— his son had to rush over there to get him. Imagine what they must have thought!"

Hugo rubbed his chin.

"Were you surprised when Mr. Groff died?" he asked bluntly.

Nurse Long grew tense. "As a matter of fact, I was." Her eyes darted between Hugo and me. "Mr. Groff's dementia was getting progressively worse, I'll admit, but he was otherwise a healthy man. His health just took a sudden turn for the worse."

"Do you or did you ever suspect that his sudden illness was unnatural in any way?" I asked.

Nurse Long shook her head adamantly. "Not at all. It seemed quite a natural death. I was just surprised because Mr. Groff was the sort of man I expected to pull through, or I suppose I'd hoped that he would. It was rough, though—he lost a lot of fluids from nausea and vomiting, and…" Nurse Long hesitated. "And, well, I think you ought to know that his nose bled."

"His nose bled?" I asked.

"That's right."

Nurse Long was quite unwavering in her statement, causing me to carefully consider the significance of her point.

"Since I heard of your arrival," she continued, her speech quickening, "I've been thinking quite a lot about Mr. Groff—trying to remember my time with him. I figured if you were going to ask me questions, I should have *something* to tell you… Well, this morning, I remembered that there *was* something that had bothered me about his death at the time, but I couldn't recall exactly what it was. I called a friend of mine, who was also there at the time of Mr. Groff's death, and he reminded me what I had found so strange." Her eyes bore into Hugo's. "It was that Mr. Groff's nose bled."

"And why is that so strange?" I asked.

"Well, it unsettled me…" she replied. "No matter how small the amount of blood, it just makes a patient's condition seem even more severe, in my opinion. And no, I guess I can't say that it's entirely strange—which was probably why it was a fleeting thought at the time—but when Mr. Groff was lying there all sick and nauseated, looking so ill…I thought, *What an odd thing, to have a nosebleed on top of it all.*"

Nurse Long shrank back in her chair, seeming a little less sure of herself. In that moment, I imagined her ever more the mouse with its thin pink ears drooping downward in embarrassment.

"I just thought—"

"Amelia, we've got to talk." A red-haired young man charged into the break room, his eyes cast downward at an open textbook he was holding. "It's just like we discussed," he continued, unaware that Hugo and I were in the room. "What I've just read, you see— Oh!" he exclaimed, finally lifting his head. Closing his textbook, he moved it behind his back and extended his free hand in greeting. "I'm sorry…I didn't mean to interrupt."

"That's all right," replied Hugo, studying the young man. "I'm Private Investigator Hugo Flynn."

The young man's eyes widened and then weighed heavily on Nurse Long. "Here to see you?"

Nurse Long stood. "It's all right."

She guided the young man through the door—rather hastily, in my opinion.

"If you will give us just a moment?" she asked apologetically, awaiting no reply.

"Strange," I remarked. "That boy seemed highly anxious— particularly at seeing you, Hugo."

Hugo didn't comment. It was moments later when Nurse Long returned, alone.

"Your brother?" asked Hugo, intrigued.

"Brother?" Nurse Long reclaimed her seat. "Oh! My brother—no." She suddenly glared at us with a discerning eye. "So you know about my brother, do you? No. That was Kyle Belton. He is the son of the custodian here at Sunny Creek. He is just a…friend."

Hugo studied her.

"He seemed quite anxious to see you," he said.

Nurse Long's expression hardened. "He has nothing to do with any of this. As I said, we are friends and he came to me with a personal matter."

I suddenly felt that our meek little mouse had vanished. Nurse Long stood, and the metal legs of her chair screeched across the floor.

"Kyle has absolutely nothing to do with...with..." She stormed from the room.

I silently conceded to Hugo's point. Perhaps she was not entirely as meek as she seemed, and I suddenly wondered if she ever did get Mr. Riley to take his pills.

≪

"Well, this is where Dr. Ballard spent much of his time volunteering," I remarked, casting an uncertain eye over the space. Situated between an ordinary cafeteria and a small stage (on which I expect many amateur productions were performed) was the activities room. Several game tables filled the area, but only one was currently being used by a couple of residents.

I wasn't sure what had so intrigued the doctor about the activities area—particularly as it related to Mr. Groff—but something must have caused him to take a sudden interest in this part of the nursing home. I expressed these thoughts to Hugo.

"Do you have any idea what Dr. Ballard was searching for here?" I asked.

Hugo lifted a lid from a checkers box, finding nothing of consequence inside.

"I can't say with certainty," he replied, "but we've learned from Ms. Helms that Mr. Groff spent much of his time here as a resident—and then the doctor, upon learning of Mr. Groff's death, decided to do the same…"

Hugo frowned, his eyes slowly moving across the room. Quite suddenly, he dropped to the linoleum floor, casting an examining eye under the game tables. I smiled uncomfortably at two elderly gentlemen playing chess; one man's finger remained frozen on his rook piece as he stared at Hugo's odd behavior.

"There must be *something*…" mumbled Hugo, standing.

As he often did when perplexed, Hugo swept his messy hair from his massive forehead, his mind churning for possible clues.

I skimmed over the various board games, all stacked on a table in a corner of the room. As I picked up a run-down deck of cards, one of the gentlemen playing chess—who I was quite certain was keeping a close eye on us at this point—called for my attention.

"Won't get much play from that, young man," he said. "Short a few cards, it is. We've got a new deck over here—we just keep those if we need to replace any of these." He patted a new deck of cards adjacent to his chessboard. "We were going to play a hand when we were done with this game, but the way Jorge's playing, we might be at this for a while!" He croaked out a laugh as his friend grunted in reply.

"This game is not for the swift, Archie—not for the swift," replied Jorge as he examined the chessboard with rapt attention.

"Of course!" yelled Hugo.

Chess pieces scattered to the floor as the two men jumped in their seats and bumped the table with their knees.

"*What?* What's wrong?" I asked, dropping the deck of cards.

"Recall the doctor's first encounter with Mr. Groff at his office," explained Hugo. "Mr. Groff asked Dr. Ballard if he could save him. That means Mr. Groff not only uncovered a specific date, he also knew that he was the one who was going to die…"

Hugo's long fingers drummed excitedly against his chest, and my arms fell to my sides as I apologized to the two men. They didn't reply. They collected their chessboard and shuffled from the room. I'm sure I heard the word "crazy" lingering on their lips.

"But it wasn't really a date, was it?" continued Hugo.

I sighed and turned back to my friend.

"It was a series of numbers that *indicated* a date," he clarified. "So, we are back to our original question, David. Why not just say the date? Why a series of numbers? It's not a natural thing to do."

Hugo spun slowly on his heel, his palms now tapping rhythmically against the pant leg of his Gucci suit. His eyes narrowed as he scrutinized the room.

"It must have been something in here." He pointed his slender fingers toward the linoleum floor. "Something in the activities center, something he *saw*… We need numbers. We need a series of numbers."

But there were no numbers, and I said so. There were tables and chairs, elderly men playing chess, elderly men not playing chess, and a wall of small wooden cubbies with the residents' names on them. There were, I noted, brightly colored flyers in each cubby. Perhaps they had numbers on them, but it seemed unlikely that they would connect to our case. I presumed that the numbers Mr. Groff came across would have to be something more permanent—a fixture of the activities center.

"They're short," I said, a sudden flush of excitement rushing over me. I held up the battered deck of cards I had so casually examined only minutes before. "All the cards aren't here," I said. "And *they've* got numbers…"

Hugo considered my idea, a grin slowly stretching across his face. My friend grasped the box of cards from my hand and stepped briskly toward the wall of wooden cubbies.

"The residents' mailboxes?" I asked.

"Mr. Groff *knew* that he was going to die," explained Hugo, his narrowed eyes darting searchingly across the rows of cubbies; each cubby had a handwritten name posted lopsidedly above it. "Which means he needed numbers *and* names…"

Hugo brushed his fingers across the mailboxes, skimming each of their contents. He peered into several cubbies before he finally stopped.

"Mr. James Lorimer," read Hugo aloud, stepping aside. "Numbers and names," he reiterated, motioning his hand toward the cubby. "Take a look."

Curious, I peered into Mr. Lorimer's cubby. Set on top of a stack of neon-pink and neon-green flyers advertising "Steak Saturdays" and "Talent Night" was a thin pile of battered playing cards. Hugo retrieved a pair of gloves from his blazer pocket and carefully gathered the cards, being careful not to disrupt the order in which they had been placed in the cubby. Laying them in a line, he noted that all were of the same suit: black spades. The order in which they appeared was as follows: *Queen, nine, Jack, seven, two, Queen, Jack, eight.*

"Look closely, David. Do you recall the date Dr. Ballard recited to us just before dying?"

"September 17, 2018," I replied, gradually beginning to see where Hugo was headed.

"What if the *Q* from the Queen cards," he said as he tapped each, "represented a zero? And the *J* from this Jack represented a one?"

I considered that idea, translating the cards to numbers in my head as Hugo suggested.

"So," I started slowly, "then the cards would read: zero, nine, one, seven, two, zero, one, eight…"

"Now apply the dashes like we did earlier on the cocktail napkin in Detective Shaw's office," instructed Hugo, his voice rising in excitement.

I lifted my head. "The date Dr. Ballard gave us before he died," I uttered. "September 17, 2018."

"Precisely."

"But why bother with the cards? What would be the point? Wouldn't a murderer just kill a man? Why leave hidden codes with dates and such?"

Hugo's voice was hushed as he advanced his theory.

"I believe this is how our murderer knew who needed to die and when," determined Hugo. "Codes are created for people to communicate secretly with each other. One person must have left eight playing cards in Mr. Groff's cubby, just like they've done here in Mr. Lorimer's, and then a second person found the cubby with the cards and made a note of the name and date that the person was meant to die."

"Just like we've discovered," I remarked.

"And just as Dr. Ballard must have discovered," said Hugo.

"So, what you're telling me," I said, "is that we probably have *two* suspects to search for now, and these cards are their way of communicating their plans for murder?"

"Absolutely. Think of it, these playing cards wouldn't stand out if found, certainly not in the *games* room, and even if someone did come across eight shabby cards, they would simply assume they had been misplaced from their box by one of those 'old dears, all muddled and confused.' No one is in this area regularly enough to notice a pattern having to do with the playing cards, *except*..." Hugo grinned.

"Except for someone like Mr. Groff who worked in here for *years*," I finished.

"Exactly," said Hugo. "Mr. Groff started to see the link. Remember, he was clever, David. He paid attention to things."

I shook my head. "I don't know, Hugo. A deck of cards... It seems a bit *too* cryptic, don't you think?"

"Codes are, in fact, meant to be cryptic, aren't they?" challenged Hugo. "Besides, it is best to be cryptic when planning a murder, don't you think?"

I couldn't argue there.

"The difference," continued Hugo, "is that we have been able to recognize the murderers' code of communication because we were already given the message—the date—by Dr. Ballard. Just consider what I'm saying," Hugo pressed. "Mr. Groff participated in the activities center for the several years that he lived here, right?"

"Yes, that's correct."

"We know that he suffered from dementia, but nevertheless, he was clever."

"That's right," I agreed. "Everyone we've interviewed has said as much."

Hugo fanned out the cards. "I suspect that during his more lucid moments, he realized the trend—a set of these old cards would appear, over the years, in different residents' mailboxes, and soon after that, they would die. I'm sure at first it meant nothing to him, but how odd it must have been for Mr. Groff to notice these old cards out of place over his many years here.

Remember, it was he who was solely in charge of distributing the newsletters and flyers to each cubby." Hugo turned excitedly toward the residents' mailboxes. "He started to figure it out, and then he saw *his* name. The cards were placed in *his* cubby."

"Not knowing who was involved here at the nursing home," I continued, excitement growing within me, "he asked Dr. Ballard if he could save him. We know that over the previous four years his cognitive functions had progressively deteriorated, so he told the doctor what he could, the best way he could, by making a note of the numbers."

"Exactly."

"Do you think he sought out Dr. Ballard specifically?" I asked.

Hugo shook his head. "I doubt it. I think Mr. Groff went to Dr. Ballard for help merely because the doctor's office was right next to the nursing home."

"So," I started slowly, considering the small wooden cubby, "that means this resident, Mr. Lorimer, is next to die?"

"He's supposed to be," replied Hugo. "But not anymore. It's time we saw Detective Shaw."

Detective Shaw closed her office door behind her.

"I don't know how you come up with these things, Mr. Flynn," she said. "If it were anyone else handing me a tattered deck of cards that are meant to suggest a hidden code, I'd tell them to take a hike, but let's see what we can make of this."

Detective Shaw lifted a sheet of paper from her desk.

"It took some time, but we've uncovered some additional information that you might find rather interesting. Of the deaths that occurred at Sunny Creek Nursing Home over the past four years, we found that seven included lofty sums of inheritance left by the deceased to a family member or members. Of those seven, however, four died of cardiac arrest." Detective Shaw paused.

"I can't imagine that's unusual," I remarked, "considering the age and various states of health of the residents."

Detective Shaw handed us copies of the report. "It wouldn't be, were it not for the small fact that each resident also had the strikingly unusual symptom of having either a bloody nose or bleeding from the eyes at the time of their death, including Mr. Groff. A strikingly unusual symptom for all to have in common, don't you think?"

Detective Shaw reclined in her chair.

"Of course, no connection was made between these deaths, since they occurred so far apart over the four-year period, but when you actually look for it, the similarity is rather alarming." Detective Shaw thumbed through another file folder on her desk. "It's also worth mentioning that Mr. Groff's son inherited a great deal of money—and just in time too. It seems he had made some poor financial decisions around the time of his father's death."

"Poison," stated Hugo. "I would suggest that there is a very strong possibility that these residents were poisoned for the inheritance they would leave behind."

"That's my line of thinking," agreed Detective Shaw.

"But what kind of poison are we talking about?" I asked. "Can't be arsenic or strychnine, or one of those other ones you often read about. Bloody noses and eyes? I've never heard of such a thing."

"No," said Hugo, "but I suspect that Nurse Long could provide us with that information."

"Nurse Long?" asked Detective Shaw. "And what does she know ab—"

"Excuse me, Detective Shaw," called a voice from behind the door.

"Come in," replied the detective.

"We've got someone here requesting to speak with you about that nursing home case—a Nurse Long."

I looked toward my friend as if he were some sort of conjurer.

Detective Shaw gave the slightest hesitation before replying. "Yes, thank you. Send her in."

Nurse Long entered slowly, pulling a few strands of her stringy hair behind her ear.

"Nurse Long," greeted Detective Shaw. "Please, have a seat."

Nurse Long nodded apprehensively.

"I had a feeling you'd come," said Hugo.

Nurse Long's eyes settled steadily on Hugo's.

"Was it rhubarb poisoning?" asked the nurse.

Detective Shaw's eyes narrowed. "Perhaps you should tell me what you know, Nurse Long."

"Of…of course. That's actually why I'm here—to help."

Digging into her bag, Nurse Long pulled out a large textbook.

"Earlier today," explained the nurse, turning the pages of the textbook hurriedly, "Kyle—Kyle Belton, that is—came to the nursing home to show me something." She looked toward Hugo and me. "You both were there."

"That's right, the red-haired boy," I said. "He seemed highly anxious."

Nurse Long flushed. "Oh, Kyle wasn't anxious because he had anything to do with Mr. Groff's death. He is just a little stressed—"

"Go on," interrupted Detective Shaw. "Tell us about the poison."

"Well, just as I told Mr. Flynn, I remembered that Mr. Groff's nose bled the day he died, and I mentioned it to Kyle at that time… It sometimes helps when I talk out loud about my work."

She looked appealingly toward Detective Shaw, who remained somber and distrustful.

"Well," Nurse Long began again, clearing her throat, "it was Kyle I called earlier, to help me recall what I had found so strange about Mr. Groff's death."

She hesitated, drawing in a deep breath.

"Kyle and I have often talked about how we can tell when a family member is just…well, there is no polite way to say this… but we can tell when a family member is just waiting for one of the residents to die. And, well, with you guys showing up, and my odd feeling about Mr. Groff…we wondered if anyone had ever tried to force God's hand, if you will."

"Murder," said Hugo.

Nurse Long's eyes grew wide, her pink mouse ears flushing a crimson hue.

"Yes…yes, that's what I mean. It all sounds so awful! But then Kyle came today, with his textbook." She placed it on Detective Shaw's desk, open to a chapter on poisons. "You see, he is studying to be a pharmacist, and his book discusses several types of poison."

Nurse Long pointed her pale finger to the text. Detective Shaw reviewed the information aloud.

"Rhubarb. It's a type of plant. The leaves contain"— Detective Shaw skimmed the notes—"oxalic acid, potassium, and calcium oxalates—not to mention a variety of other toxins."

She lifted her head. "It's really the leaves that are poisonous, but if you were to cook the leaf blades into someone's food, it would serve as a nasty digestive irritant—nausea, vomiting, and, uniquely, bleeding from the nose or eyes…" A corner of Detective Shaw's mouth lifted. "Eventually, the calcium content of the blood drops, and the person goes into cardiac or respiratory arrest."

"Kyle saw the symptoms in his textbook," said Nurse Long. "Rhubarb poisoning can cause a bloody nose—Mr. Groff had a bloody nose, and he was certainly nauseous." She looked appealingly toward Hugo. "And, well, I never did think Mr. Groff's son cared much for his father…" Her voice trailed off.

"So," remarked Hugo as he scrubbed at a scuff on his dress shoe. "That's that."

Detective Shaw looked toward me, but I just shook my head.

"Is it?" she asked Hugo. "That's that?"

Hugo's eyes moved searchingly between Detective Shaw and me. He appeared puzzled.

"Hugo," I started, leaning toward my friend so he could focus. "Please explain *aloud* what you are thinking."

"Oh! Well, isn't that clear? The case, of course, and the fact that it's solved." Hugo straightened. "Didn't I say?"

I was pleased when, for the first time, the beautiful Detective Shaw cast me an amused glance.

"Well, that's that," she repeated, her dark curls bouncing across her shoulders as she shook her head, marveling at my friend.

I admit that I, too, found some amusement in my friend's inability to understand that the world did not equally possess his genius mind.

Nurse Long shifted uncomfortably in her chair. "You mean Mr. Flynn knows?" she asked. "Who…who killed Mr. Groff?"

"Absolutely, Nurse Long," replied Hugo. "He was murdered by the nursing home's cook, and that custodian fellow, Matthew Belton. Oh! But I suppose you just know him as your friend Kyle's dad."

Nurse Long's face paled, which was swiftly followed by a soft thud that echoed through Detective Shaw's office.

"Walters!" yelled Detective Shaw, rushing toward Nurse Long, who had fainted and fallen from her chair. A uniformed officer hurried in. "Quick! Get me a glass of water."

"*Hugo*," I mumbled, helping to collect Nurse Long from the floor.

Hugo scratched his head. "Something I said?"

❧

"What made you suspect the custodian, Matthew Belton?" I asked as Hugo and I returned home.

Hugo hung up his coat before settling onto the sofa.

"A couple things," he said, sliding a pillow under his head. "First, the simple fact that Mr. Belton worked two jobs. I knew he needed money, and when it comes to murder investigations, it's always good to make a note of who could do with a bit more income—possible motive."

"Drink?" I asked.

"Please, water." He continued. "It really started to make sense to me when we found the playing cards. That's when I realized that there must be two individuals communicating with each other— Thanks."

Hugo pushed himself up, accepting the glass from my hand.

"One murderer," he explained, "was in charge of determining

the date and person they would murder, while the other was responsible for actually carrying it out. Mr. Belton worked only evening shifts and only had access to the public areas. Therefore, he couldn't go into the private rooms, but he did have access to places like the activities center. I also found it interesting that he was quite sociable with the visitors, and if Nurse Long and Kyle could make a note of which family members wanted their loved ones 'out of the way,' then so could Mr. Belton."

"You mean he was 'sociable' with the visitors to see who would require his…murdering services…?"

"Precisely, David!"

"I'm going to ask that you be a bit less excited by this, Hugo."

"Oh right." Hugo nodded. "So, like I said, Mr. Belton is talkative with the visitors, mainly to feel them out. He determines who has a less-than-honorable interest in their 'loved' one's health, and he decides to meet with those particular individuals—subtly making suggestions at first, until their discussion ultimately leads to determining a date upon which that resident will be murdered. As payment, I assume he and his accomplice, the cook, received a percentage of the inheritance."

Hugo took another sip of water.

"Did you notice that the cafeteria is adjacent to the activities area?" asked Hugo. "The cook is a likely suspect for two main reasons. First, she is close enough to the activities center to look casually for the cards without anyone thinking much of her presence there. After all, her kitchen is right next door. She simply had to wander over and make a note of who needed to be murdered and when."

"But how do you know the cook had anything to do with it?

Just because the cafeteria is near to the activities center doesn't mean that she had any involvement."

"That brings us to my second reason for suspecting the cook. As a matter of fact, it was Nurse Long who inadvertently brought her to my attention," recalled Hugo. "She mentioned that Mr. Groff received an extra dessert from the cook on his dinner tray. Nurse Long assumed it was because Mr. Groff and the cook got along. In reality, it was because she was lacing the food with poisonous leaves."

Hugo was quiet for a moment and then added, with just the slightest hint of admiration, "It's really quite clever. The cook and Mr. Belton never even had to interact—at least not in a way that others would notice. They could have appeared to be virtual strangers to others looking on."

"But why set such a specific date?" I asked.

"Do you recall what Detective Shaw said? Over the four years, those who died under suspicious circumstances were never connected because their deaths were spaced so far apart. If the murderers had arranged five bloody noses in one year, people would have started to wonder. But no more than one bloody nose a year, and no one makes the connection."

"It was strategic."

"I'm sure of it," agreed Hugo. "Plus, I'm almost certain the people who desired their inheritance prematurely did so because they needed the money. A date would guarantee a time frame in which they'd get paid."

I shuddered at the wickedness of it all.

"Poor Dr. Ballard," I remarked. "He must have found out."

Hugo nodded. "The doctor started to put the pieces together, having made several visits to the facility to investigate, under the guise of volunteering. I presume he suspected the custodian for reasons not unlike my own. Perhaps, determined to confirm his suspicions, he went back to investigate the nursing home while the custodian or the cook were working, but one of them found out about him first. He tried to escape and was shot, but he got far enough to reach our doorstep. When we found him, he was dying from his gunshot wound, but he knew that if he could make me remember what we had previously discussed, I might solve the case—or better yet, *cases*—of the murders at the nursing home and his own murder. Fortunately, it worked."

"Doctors save lives, and he has lost his because of this."

In that moment, I felt Hugo's cynicism was quite justified.

"And Kyle?" I asked, picturing that anxious young man. "Did he know about his dad's involvement, and that's why he acted so nervous when he saw us? Not to mention how anxious he appeared to Ms. Helms as well."

"Oh no! Not at all," said Hugo, moving to his piano. "He had no idea about his dad's role in the murders, or where his dad obtained the money to pay for his schooling. I suspect he was just anxious because he had been getting illegal stimulants from Nurse Long to make it through his school finals."

My jaw dropped as Hugo ran his fingers across the ivory. Suddenly stilling, he turned toward me.

"I suppose we should also mention that to Detective Shaw?"

"Probably," I replied, masking my amusement. "She would probably want to at least look into your theory."

Hugo nodded. Turning once more to his piano, he played an original composition as I spread myself across the sofa.

"And that's that," I said, falling into a much-needed sleep.

Amazon Kindle 9780996521024
eBook 9780996521031
Paperback 9780996521017
Hardcover 9780996521000

ALSO AVAILABLE

THE HOTEL WESTEND: A MYSTERY

At the historic Hotel Westend, murder—like history—has a tendency to repeat itself.

When the timid yet curious Elsie Maitland stumbles upon a small, seaside town, she takes a room in the lone hotel on top of the cliffs—but something's amiss. A curious group of guests has been assembled by an unknown host, but what's even more puzzling is that not even the guests seem to know why. What they do know, however, is that they were all suspects in an unsolved murder twenty years earlier, a murder that took place at this very hotel. History soon repeats itself when an unassuming reverend is bludgeoned to death and the hotel's maid is poisoned, leaving the guests to wonder, who's next?

"A charming homage to the classic mystery… Lynch-Harris playfully indulges genre tropes, raising readers' suspicions equally among multiple characters."

- Publishers Weekly

"This solidly plotted story kept me glued to the pages until I finally reached the very satisfying solution to the mystery."

– Jack Magnus, *Readers' Favorite*

EXCERPT

THE HOTEL WESTEND

CHAPTER 1

THE GUESTS

I

Shifting his weight, Amos Hartin groaned as the less inflamed of his knees sank into the grassy plain. Peering through wide-set eyes, the hotel's elderly gardener tilted his long face downward and pressed his shovel into the soil.

"Unusual is what it is," Amos grumbled through small, pinched lips. He tugged a weed free from the soil, his bottom lip pursed in defiance. "An entire group of guests arriving and I've only just found out…"

He frowned, counting seven chrysanthemums still in their planters.

"No," he murmured decidedly. "Doesn't leave me much time at all."

The elderly man lifted his head as a commanding gust of wind swept toward him from the sea. The Hotel Westend was built on a plateau of rock that jutted out over the massive body of water; it had sheer cliffs on three of its sides. Dragging his sleeve across his brow, Amos peered at a lone seagull that squawked loudly overhead, competing with the waves' ballad strumming against the rocks below.

Amos sighed and shook his head firmly. "I'll just have to do what I can."

Drawing in a deep breath, he gave his shovel another quick, shaky thrust and plunged it deeper into the ground. This time, however, his eyebrows rose.

"Now what is *this*...?"

With a sudden burst, his spade broke through the earth and a soft thud resonated from the caked dirt that fell beside him. Gingerly he brushed his fingers over the soil and with each stroke his forehead wrinkled like a curious bloodhound.

"My goodness," he uttered, reaching for what appeared to be a dark medicine bottle. Amos glanced around but saw no one. He pinched the bottle between his fingertips and lifted it carefully above his head. The gardener turned it to and fro, watching as several pill capsules tumbled over each other.

II

The only coffee shop in Westend Bay, Gull's Café, was situated on the main street of the town, just a mile and a half from the hotel. Two women were seated outside the café, each talking on her phone without a care in the world. Inside the café was the inquisitive Mrs. Vesta Tidwell, who, in the town's opinion, often cared a bit *too* much about other people's personal affairs. Today it was the morning edition of the *Westend Gazette* that garnered Mrs. Tidwell's undivided attention.

"Well, *well*," she murmured from her corner table. "What would a *millionaire* have to do with our humble little town?"

"More pie, Mrs. Tidwell?" Lisette, the waitress, asked.

Lowering the *Gazette*, the older woman nodded.

"Have you heard, Lisette?" asked Mrs. Tidwell, brushing a stray curl from above her eye. "We've got some wealthy visitors arriving in our quaint little community—and staying at the Hotel Westend, no less."

"So I've heard, ma'am," confirmed Lisette with fashioned interest.

"I wonder what they will be like…"

Lisette smiled. "And how are your arm and your leg today, Mrs. Tidwell?"

Mrs. Tidwell looked puzzled for a moment.

"Oh!" She exhaled. "The doctor insists that I continue to wear these dreaded casts. He assures me he can remove them soon, but I can't get anywhere without help! *Complete* torture!"

Mrs. Tidwell fell some weeks ago from a rusty ladder in her back yard and broke an arm and a leg, a testament to the dangers of trimming the branches of one's apple tree. Most couldn't help but notice that, at the time of Mrs. Tidwell's disastrous incident, Mr. Humphreys and his *mistress*, Ms. Sanders, were said to have been arguing in the upstairs bedroom of the adjacent house. This, incidentally, was next to the open window…which was, of course, near to a large and now tragically asymmetrical apple tree. Needless to say, it was quite fortunate for Mrs. Tidwell that Norma Kemper, the Tidwells' longtime maid, had returned to the house in search of her watch and discovered her fallen employer instead.

"And *this*!" murmured Mrs. Tidwell to herself (for Lisette had shrewdly taken her leave). She raised the *Gazette* and frowned. "How—just *how*, in my condition, am I going to scale the steep gravel drive to the hotel?"

At the chime of the café's door, Mrs. Tidwell propped herself up with her good arm and swiftly turned her small, pointed nose toward the entryway, proving that her predatory instincts were still in good working order.

"Doris!" she called. "Doris!"

Mrs. Doris Malford, the local florist, nodded her head vigorously, her small, feathered hat sliding askew as she maneuvered excitedly between the small tables to her friend.

"Have you seen the *Gazette*?" asked Mrs. Tidwell.

"Indeed I have, Vesta," replied Mrs. Malford keenly, taking a seat. "Indeed I *have*. But have you seen the *Tribune*?"

Handing her friend the paper, she smiled broadly. Mrs. Tidwell's eyebrows rose. A mammoth-sized photo sat beneath the headline:

MILLIONAIRE RICHARD WELLING MARRIED

"My husband picked up a copy at the train station on his way back from Glassden," whispered Mrs. Malford conspiringly. "Isn't it something!"

"He has to be at *least* twice her age!" exclaimed Mrs. Tidwell. "Just *look* at her!"

Leaning forward, she smoothed the paper against the table. "Goodness, Doris!" She lifted her head. "He married an infant."

Mrs. Malford sighed. "It's like what you see in movies or read about in books, isn't it?" she considered thoughtfully, helping herself to a slice of pie. "I suppose it's like winning the lottery. Or finding a pearl in an oyster."

Mrs. Tidwell lifted the *Tribune* once more and skimmed the article. "My *goodness*," she uttered from behind the paper. As she shook her head, strands of frazzled, wispy gray hair fell free from her bun. Mrs. Malford nodded appreciatively as Lisette placed a cup of tea on the table.

"There was no pre-nup!" declared Mrs. Tidwell, turning the page ravenously.

Mrs. Malford nodded vigorously. "Like an oyster!" she reiterated somewhat indistinctly, owing to a mouth full of pie. "Like finding an unbelievably *massive* pearl in an oyster!"

The steady rumble of a car's engine moved slowly past the café. Turning, Mrs. Malford peered through the large front windows. Her blue eyes widened.

"Vesta, that's *her*."

"What's that, Doris? Oh!" exclaimed Mrs. Tidwell, stumbling upon yet another photograph. "Just *look* at their estate!"

"Mrs. *Olivia Welling*," choked Mrs. Malford as she followed the silver Rolls-Royce with her eyes. "She's in the *car*, Vesta!"

Mrs. Tidwell looked up sharply, her mouth slightly ajar as she gazed intently ahead. A young woman in her thirties, with short black hair slicked down against her fair skin, sat comfortably in the plush luxury of hand-stitched leather seats.

"They must be headed up to the hotel now," whispered Mrs. Malford, tapping the *Gazette* decisively. "Right here, in our very own town! Imagine what a millionaire's life must be like," she remarked dreamily.

Held captive to the seat by her bulky casts, a faint whimper escaped Mrs. Tidwell as she realized that imagining was indeed all she could do.

"Isn't it something, Doris?" she remarked, reclining as the Rolls-Royce thundered away. "They can do anything they like—visit anywhere in the world, buy all the homes they want and all the clothes they like and…"

Mrs. Tidwell's voice faded. Mrs. Malford lifted her eyes curiously over the rim of her tea cup.

"Vesta?"

Drawn back into the conversation, Mrs. Tidwell remarked, "Say, that's a point, isn't it?"

Mrs. Malford replaced her cup in its saucer. "What is, dear?"

"The Wellings," said Mrs. Tidwell thoughtfully. "They *can* go anywhere in the world."

"That's right…"

Mrs. Tidwell looked at her friend.

"So why come here?"

III

Meanwhile in New York City, seated in the corner of her front sitting room, Iradene Hartwell sat upright on the plush cushion of her antique wingback chair surrounded by rich furnishings and heavy draperies. Layered in a purple brocade dress and a silver wrap that rested squarely over her shoulders, the fifty-one-year-old socialite waited impatiently for her car, resenting her upcoming trip.

"*Wretched letter!*" she uttered aloud, discreetly unfolding the ivory stationery between her fingertips. Again she read the note.

Dear Ms. Hartwell,

I hope this note finds you well. It has been quite a while, hasn't it? The last time we saw each other was at the Hotel Westend twenty years ago! Oh! How foolish of me. You undoubtedly remember it as the McCrays' old residence,

Westend Manor. My my, where has the time gone—and yet somehow it seems like only yesterday, doesn't it? Amazing how one can't remember the silliest things from just days ago while some things one never forgets. That brings me to my little idea. I thought how marvelous it would be if we had a sort of reunion. What do you think, Ms. Hartwell? We could reminisce about all that happened.

With that being said, I'd love for you to join us, as I know you certainly wouldn't want someone else to speak for you. One must be so careful of one's reputation nowadays, mustn't one? People say the strangest things…

Iradene lifted her eyes as the sound of hurried footsteps came to a stop just outside the doorway.

"Iradene," said a softly spoken voice.

She turned her face toward the door; it was a strikingly unattractive face with pale, sunken cheeks and puckered, fish-like lips.

"You're late. Where have you been?" she demanded of her far younger sister.

Marian Hartwell cast her eyes downward.

"I—I've just finished loading the car, Iradene. We are all ready to go now."

"It certainly took you long enough. Make sure that you have our travel papers in order."

Marian glanced briefly at the itinerary in her hand and silently read over the gold-embossed lettering at the top of the page: "Skylark Travel Agency". With only the subtlest lift of her chin, she confirmed, "Yes, everything is already arranged."

Without responding, Iradene's gaze darted dismissively from

her sister to the window. As she rested her small, dark eyes on her garden, she caught a glimpse of what appeared to be a man's figure disappearing beyond the garden wall.

Annoyed, she pulled back her velvet drapes and leaned forward. She scanned the grounds again but saw nothing. And yet…

Strange, thought the older woman. *I could have sworn there was somebody out there.*

IV

With only 20 minutes left until he reaches the Hotel Westend, James Rennick sat contentedly in the first-class carriage of the train, thoroughly absorbed in the *Tribune's* daily crossword. Lifting the round frames of his glasses, he rubbed absently at the bridge of his nose and quietly muttered various six-letter words.

"Hidden…H-I-D-D… No, no." He shook his head. "That won't do."

His eyes scanned from left to right, moving unhurriedly across the page.

"Maybe covert?" he mumbled. "C-O-V… No."

He straightened. A toothy grin spread across his face.

"*Secret*. S-E-C-R-E-T."

He drew his pen and filled in the empty spaces.

"Yes, that's it."

Satisfied, he laid the paper down and glanced through the window. Night was approaching as the seaside came into view; a gray hue hovered over the restless waves in the distance. A quick look at his watch revealed that it had already been forty-five minutes. *Funny*, he thought, *that I've never visited Westend Bay although I've lived such a short distance away all these years.*

James's body leaned gently against the window as the train curved swiftly around a bend. He suddenly realized he felt very tired. It had been quite some time since he had had a day off, let alone *two weeks*. Journalists didn't take time off, he had decided long ago, at least not if they wanted to move ahead. He had been just an intern then, though. Now he had his own column and he'd already had a few breaking stories. His position was secure enough to have this time away.

James drew in a deep breath, smiling as he remembered the invitation: "We at Bookworm Puzzles are happy to inform you that you've won the grand prize—an all-expense paid vacation to the Hotel Westend! Please see the attached for details. Thank you for entering."

Yes, it was good timing—that letter—and all expenses paid at that! First-class carriage, a seaside vacation, and all from my silly little hobby.

James's brows wrinkled forward.

Still can't remember entering that contest, though…

He blinked tiredly, peering once more through the window. It was night now.

Strange how darkness can mask such a massive body of water; and yet it would be foolish to think that it somehow wasn't there— that it would have just gone away.

James yawned, shifting in his seat.

"Some things will never go away," he muttered.

Closing his eyes, he drifted off to sleep.

V

Paul Hulling thumbed absently through a dog-eared copy of *Middlemarch*. Casting an anxious glance at his watch, he replaced the book on its shelf and peered toward the front doors of the New York Public Library.

Davis still hadn't arrived.

"Perhaps I shouldn't go through with this," he murmured, shrinking back behind the bookcase. "Something hasn't felt right about this whole plan from the beginni—"

Paul's cheeks reddened as he caught sight of an olive-skinned woman with dark, curly hair at the end of the aisle. She lifted her head curiously, smiling gently in his direction. Clearing his throat, he turned his attention to a set of novels, dragging his finger across their spines as he wandered discreetly toward the next bookcase.

His eyes lingered once more on the door and he flinched as his phone vibrated in his suit jacket.

"Hello?"

"Paul, it's Davis."

Paul slid further into the aisle.

"Where *are* you?" he hissed. "I was just debating whether I should forget this whole idea."

"Well, don't. And remember, *you* called me into all this."

Paul considered the man on the other end before replying.

"All right. Where would I have to go?"

"A small town by the name of Westend Bay. I hope you like water."

Paul didn't answer. Wearily he rubbed at his eyes.

"I don't see that you have any other options," said Davis. "I did my part, now you do yours."

Paul drew in a breath. "Who do I need to contact?"

"Skylark Travel Agency. A travel package has already been arranged. Your flight leaves in five hours."

Paul bit at his lip and nodded. "I better get packed."

There was a thick silence. Just as Paul was wondering whether Davis had gone, the man's voice broke in once more.

"Handle this, Paul."

Davis hesitated a moment but went on.

"Look," he started slowly, his voice gruff. "I've got a feeling it's only going to get worse. It's *already* getting worse. You *have* to handle this."

Again there was silence.

Paul glanced at his phone and confirmed that, this time, the line had indeed gone dead.

VI

Elsie Maitland cut a sharp right and pressed a bit more on the gas, her small rental car wheezing as it traversed the steep, winding road toward the Hotel Westend.

"Oh, bother—oh, bother…" she murmured, carefully maneuvering the car between the iron fencing that lined the cliff edge and the high hedges that lined the other side of the road.

Elsie winced as the engine groaned, puffing unmistakably, "I think I can, I think I can". She seriously debated whether her little locomotive really could. Pulling the wheel in the other direction, she gave a firm push on the accelerator and the car lurched forward onto level ground. Slowing her speed, the bookstore owner eased her car across the gravel drive and pulled it to a jerky stop outside the hotel.

"'Just up the hill'," she mimicked, sliding her slender legs from the car. "'*Sure* your car can make it! The old hotel is *just* up top.'" Elsie slammed the driver's door. "'Nowadays, hatchbacks are sturdier than you think!'

"Ha!"

As she retrieved her luggage, a warm mix of light and shadows washed across her smooth, brown skin.

"Just nearly sunset," she noted as a breeze swept toward her.

The green ivy climbing the hotel's stone walls fluttered gently, and the wind pulled strands of her hair from the French braid that drew snugly into a bun at the base of her neck.

Glancing at her watch, Elsie drew a deep breath and looked around. Reflexively, as was so often her habit when curious, her small, round nose bobbed up and down, gently lifting her especially thick green frames. She peered admiringly at the full-sized tennis court, which sat further off to one side of the hotel, and the chrysanthemums that lined the border of its stone walls.

"Hotel Westend," she murmured, eyeing the old wooden sign that swayed gently above the hotel's doorway.

Pulling the few wayward hairs behind her ear, Elsie collected her luggage and approached the hotel's entrance. One of two huge, antique oak doors opened, revealing the short, square build of the hotel manager. Stepping forward, his dark eyes darted watchfully behind Elsie before he finally set his owl-like face upon her. He gave a short, dry cough.

"Good afternoon, ma'am. My name is Mr. Dennis Needling. May I help you?"

"Yes, please." Elsie shifted her luggage to her side. "I'll need a room. I've gotten a bit lost. The grocer—a Mr. Reginald Glover, I believe it was—directed me here. He said you're the only hotel in town?"

Mr. Needling gave another dry cough. "That's right—" He hesitated. "Where exactly were you trying to go?"

"Oh!"

Elsie patted her pockets.

"Right. I'm afraid I'm often in the habit of losing things." She frowned and sifted through the contents of her purse. "Oh bother," she murmured, resting her hands atop her hips. "The place was a sort of bird…" She waved her painted fingernails over her head arbitrarily.

"A bird?" questioned Mr. Needling.

"Right. A pelican? A crane?"

He shook his head.

"All day you know the name of a place, but then it just suddenly slips your mind!" she exclaimed, unzipping the top compartment of her black and white-striped luggage.

Scatterbrained, thought Mr. Needling irritably.

Elsie had always been a uniquely clever woman, but one whose first impression was often marred by minor bouts of forgetfulness and disorganization. Nevertheless she carried herself with great dignity, but she was most often noticed for her selection of glasses, which had exceptionally large frames that varied in color and shape.

"Ah!"

Mr. Needling straightened, forcing a smile as Elsie unfolded a crinkled sheet of paper and quickly skimmed it over.

"Eagle's Point," she said, leveling her eyes with his.

Mr. Needling's breath caught in his throat.

"Like I said—a bird," she went on, shrugging.

Sharp eyes, he concluded silently. *Very clever, this one.*

He cleared his throat. "Eagle's Point, you say?" Squinting,

he made note of the time on his watch. "No, no. That won't do; I can't arrange it in time." He sighed, peering past her.

Funny little man, thought Elsie. *Anxious like a cat.*

Mr. Needling turned his gaze abruptly on her, as though she had said the words aloud. Stepping forward, he collected her bag. "You'll need a room," he remarked. "If you'll come this way…"

Situated just beyond an old grandfather clock was the reception desk.

"That's Mr. Elbert Turnbull, our only permanent resident," whispered Mr. Needling, nodding his head toward a spacious sitting area just across from the reception desk. Facing the marble fireplace and comfortably situated in one of two wing-back chairs was a stout older gentleman, his head drooping gently to one side. The old man stirred in his chair.

"He's been a sort of long-standing guest of ours," explained Mr. Needling.

Mr. Turnbull's slack chin quivered and a faint whistle drifted upward from his lips, only to be immediately followed by two successive sniffs.

Mr. Needling continued. "The owner of our little hotel has made arrangements for Mr. Turnbull to stay here. He's become sort of a fixture of our establishment, if you will."

"If you'll just sign here, please," he instructed, collecting a key from the wall behind him. "I'm glad we could provide you accommodations," he said, nodding forward. "Please, this way."

He rushed ahead in quick, short steps across the dark, hardwood floor.

"I'm the hotel manager," he explained, looking at Elsie from the side of his eye.

"I'm Elsie Maitland."

"*Yes*," remarked Mr. Needling thoughtfully. He gave another dry cough. "I gathered that when you signed in."

Casting a furtive glance at the manager, Elsie made no reply but followed behind Mr. Needling as he ascended the oak and iron stairway. Arriving on the large landing, he turned and guided her down a long hall of doors.

"Mr. Turnbull seems quite comfortable," said Elsie.

Mr. Needling gave a breathless laugh and turned.

"Your room, Ms. Maitland," he said, pushing the door open. "You should know that the hotel actually used to be a personal residence," he explained, depositing Elsie's luggage beside the four poster bed, "but it has been years since the family…left."

Elsie listened with peaked interest as Mr. Needling continued.

"The home was soon converted into a hotel and, as a result, we have a beautiful dining hall in which we host dinner for our guests every evening at the same time: 6 pm. I'm afraid dinner has already concluded for *this* evening, but I can certainly—"

"No, that's all right," interrupted Elsie. "I'm actually a bit tired. I plan to turn in."

"Very well, Ms. Maitland. Please let me know if you need anything at all."

Mr. Needling skulked from the room and closed the door behind him.

"What a strange little man," murmured Elsie.

؏

As night descended upon the hotel, Elsie Maitland took a seat at the cherry writing desk near to her window. Drawing the curtains, she listened to the waves as they crashed steadily against the cliffs below. She pulled a sheet of stationery from her bag and wrote:

Dear Frances,

I'm so glad I finally have a moment to write you. I love this idea you've come up with—that we should send each other letters instead of calling. Imagine if Jane Austen never left behind the letters she wrote to her sister. Imagine what little we would know about her life. It would have been a literary tragedy!

Yes, yes, I know. You have heard my stance on this, and as such I will move on to the point of this letter. As you know, I intended to travel to Eagle's Point to fulfill your fanatical request that I climb that ridiculous mountain in the shape of an eagle's head. Unfortunately—or fortunately, I'd say—I've stumbled across some other small town instead. I believe it's called Westend Bay. Apparently, the two places are hours apart, and no, I don't know how I managed it! One turn looks just like another.

Anyway, Franny, this town has got one grocer, one florist, one post office, one hotel…oh! Speaking of which, I almost died trying to drive my little rental car up the steep slope that leads to the hotel's entrance! Really, they've only got one road to get here. The other three sides are sheer cliffs leading directly into the water, with perhaps a few rocks below that you could probably walk on—if the tide were low enough, that is.

I did make note, however, of a small walking path that's got a railing beside it. I think I'll walk that route into town in the morning.

The room is nice. It overlooks the sea, but, I must admit, the hotel manager seems a bit...strange. I can't put my finger on it, but he definitely seems anxious about something— although some people are just like that, I suppose. The hotel itself is nice though. It used to be someone's home at one time. I'm sure there is plenty of history in a place like this. The architecture alone is beautiful, and the seaside is relaxing. I think I will spend a bit of time here—anything to avoid that ridiculous bird mountain!

How are things on your end? Did you find a new home healthcare worker? Hopefully she is more personable than your last. Tell Mom and Dad hello for me. Have they come back from Jamaica yet? If so, ask them if they brought me some of Grandma's coconut drops, and don't eat them this time!

I've got to get some sleep, Franny. I will write you again soon.

Love always,

—Elsie

VII

The manager of the Hotel Westend picked up the phone receiver.

"Good evening, Hotel Weste— Oh, it's you."

Mr. Needling closed the door to his office.

"Yes, I can hear you all right—it's my private line. Wait, what do you mean?"

He listened intently. It was after a few moments that he spoke again.

"Fine. I will be expecting your call. Also, we do have a few…" he paused, "…a few *unexpected* guests, but I can't imagine that they will be a problem. After all, we anticipated this as a strong possibility and nothing has to change."

Mr. Needling nodded.

"Yes, I've got it right here," he replied.

Opening the hotel guest book, he skimmed its pages.

"There is one more coming by train, but everyone else has checked in. Yes, that's right…"

Mr. Needling slid the guest book away from himself.

"No—no questions. Ok, now. Goodnight."

Hanging up the receiver, he sank slowly into his leather desk chair. Resting his hands across his chest, he thoughtfully considered the guest list.

"'Will you walk into my parlor?' said the Spider to the Fly," he mumbled quietly.

Shaking his head, he turned off the light and awaited the remaining guest.

A NOTE FROM THE AUTHOR

Dear Reader,

I hope you've enjoyed this collection of mystery stories. As you undoubtedly noticed, a few of my stories were set in locations outside of the United States. I'm often inspired by the people I meet and the places I've had the pleasure to visit. My mother and I took a trip to England recently and stayed at Bovey Castle. I fell in love with both the beautiful countryside and the excellent accommodations. It isn't surprising, then, that I found myself revisiting this delightful place through my storytelling. However, that's just it—"The Mystery at Bovey Castle" is a story. Although the setting is wonderfully real, the historical details I incorporated into the story—the regiment that landed in Egypt, the use of Bovey Castle by the fictional Hugo Avery to hide the jeweled scarab beetle, the discovery of the treasure, and so on—were purely fictitious and written specifically for my plot.

I also took some liberties with "Tamarind Lodge," which is set in beautiful Lucea, Jamaica. The hotel in which Harrington Finch stayed (and after which this story was named) did exist, but many years ago. My father would tell me stories of the time he spent as a young boy in Lucea, where he lived when he attended boarding school at the young age of twelve. Back then, Tamarind Lodge was a quaint, thriving hotel, but when my parents took me to visit many years later, only the steps remained. As such, "Tamarind Lodge" was written based on what my father shared from his memories.

Similarly, the lively character of Jo Jo Durant was actually based on a real person my father knew during that time. "Jo Jo" was wonderfully mischievous, and my brother and I grew up hearing all about his misadventures, so it was only fitting that he should be part of the story as well!

It's always a joy to create new characters and see them come to life on the page. However, as much as I love spending time in their worlds, I also enjoy getting to know the readers in ours. I hope you will connect with me via my website, AshleyLynchHarris.com, or send me an email at Contact@ AshleyLynchHarris.com.

In my book, *The Hotel Westend: A Mystery*, my two amateur sleuths—Elsie and Frances—are sisters who (still, in this day and age) write letters to each other! I gave them this shared interest because I, too, believe that there is something special about exchanging handwritten letters. If you also enjoy writing letters, my mailing address is: PO Box 47803, Tampa, Florida 33646. I will be sure to respond in kind!

Finally, if you enjoyed *A Deadly Referral and Other Mystery Stories*, I'd love for you to tell your family and friends about it, and if you have some extra time, I hope you will also post a review.

Thanks again for reading!

Sincerely,

Ashley

ABOUT THE AUTHOR

Ashley Lynch-Harris is the author of *The Hotel Westend: A Mystery*, and her short stories have been published in the *Sherlock Holmes Mystery Magazine* and *Black Cat Mystery Magazine*. When she's not writing, Ashley enjoys spending time with family and friends, watching *I Love Lucy*, and studying God's Word. Ashley is a member of the International Association of Crime Writers (North American branch) and an honors graduate of the University of South Florida. Currently, she is pursuing a Master of Fine Arts in Writing and lives in Tampa with her husband, Alex, and dog, Jo Jo.

Connect with Ashley:

Please take a moment to sign up for my occasional email updates, including new release information and exclusive giveaways. AshleyLynchHarris.com/contact

More Books by Ashley:

AshleyLynchHarris.com/books

CPSIA information can be obtained
at www.ICGtesting.com
Printed in the USA
LVHW091105071019
633401LV00005B/777/P